Finders Keepers

Chinkapin Series Book 2

I0601938

Margaret Rodeheaver

Pares Forma Press

MACON, GEORGIA

Pares Forma Press/Will Way Books
212 Will Way
Byron, Georgia 31008
www.MargaretRodeheaver.com

Publisher's Note: This is a work of fiction. Names, characters, places, and incidents are a product of the author's imagination or are used fictitiously. Locales and public names are sometimes used for atmospheric purposes. Any resemblance to actual people, living or dead, or to businesses, companies, events, institutions, or locales is completely coincidental.

Book Layout ©2017 BookDesignTemplates.com
Book Cover Design by 100 Covers

Ordering Information:
Quantity sales. Special discounts are available on quantity purchases by bookstores, associations, libraries, and others. For details, contact Will Way Books at the address above.

Finders Keepers/ Margaret Rodeheaver. -- 1st ed.
Print ISBN 978-1-7332880-0-2
Large Print ISBN 978-1-7332880-5-7
EBook ISBN 978-1-7332880-1-9

Also by Margaret Rodeheaver

Hidden Treasure (Chinkapin Series Book 1)
Second Home (Chinkapin Series Book 3)

Middle-grade books in the *Porkington's World* series:

Porkington Hamm
Porkington Returns
Bonny's Debut
Porkington Hamm and the Lost Gold
Christmas Hamm: How Porkington Found the Holiday Spirit
Porkington Hamm and the Killer Tomatoes

Middle-grade books in the *Grimsly Ghost* series:

Haunted Holiday - A Christmas Cookie Ghost Story
The Ghost at Goblin's Glen

Contents

Chapter 1...1

Chapter 2...11

Chapter 3...17

Chapter 4...25

Chapter 5...33

Chapter 6...41

Chapter 7...47

Chapter 8...55

Chapter 9...61

Chapter 10. 67

Chapter 11. 79

Chapter 12. 85

Chapter 13. 91

Chapter 14. 103

Chapter 15. 113

Chapter 16. 123

Chapter 17. 135

Chapter 18.. 145

Chapter 19.. 163

Chapter 20.. 177

Chapter 21.. 189

Chapter 22.. 197

Chapter 23.. 213

Chapter 24.. 223

Chapter 25.. 233

Chapter 26.. 243

Chapter 27.. 255

Chapter 28.. 261

Chapter 29.. 275

Chapter 30.. 285

Chapter 31.. 291

Chapter 32.. 303

Chapter 33.. 309

Chapter 34.. 319

Chapter 35.. 329

Chapter 1.

Laurie Lanton sat at the kitchen table of her little apartment ignoring the almost-suppertime growling of her stomach and pressed a few keys on her laptop. She click, click, clicked and then scrolled down the screen.

Her friends all knew she wrote for the local newspaper, and would have guessed Laurie was hard at work on another feature article. Actually she was searching an online house-hunting site, looking for historic homes near Chinkapin, Georgia.

Laurie missed the beautiful house she'd lived in up north a lot more than she ever missed the ex-husband she had shared it with. But instead of a sleek modern house like the one she had, this time around she wanted something completely different. And Georgia certainly had its share of gorgeous old houses just full of southern charm. She was ready to find one and make it her own, even if it took some work to whip it into shape.

She figured a lot of the whipping could be handled by her boyfriend Chase. They were an item, although they'd really only been together for six months. She knew her heart, and she knew Chase. And Chase was good with his hands. Boy, was he ever. Laurie spent a distracted moment thinking about just how good he was with his hands.

But Chase Harris was also a great handyman. And if he couldn't do it himself, he could find a tradesman who could. He had become acquainted with a lot of excellent tradesmen since he started working at Anderson's HVAC Company.

Laurie's cell phone dinged. She saved a picture of the latest house she'd fallen in love with, and snapped her laptop shut. Then she grabbed her phone and keys and ran down the stairs to the first floor.

Chase and Laurie lived in the same apartment building, across the tracks from Chinkapin's more picturesque historic neighborhoods. There was nothing special about their apartments, but they were affordable, and convenient to where each of them worked, and to St. Mark's Episcopal Church, where the two had met in the choir loft. They sometimes talked about letting one of the apartments go, but Laurie liked having her own closet, her own bathroom, and her own place to get away and write. She was her own woman, and had gotten used to making her own decisions and living life on her terms.

Luckily Chase was not the kind of guy who cramped her style.

She knocked on his door, and opened it without waiting for an answer. "I'm here," she called.

Chase appeared from behind the door of the open refrigerator. He set a package containing a roasted chicken onto the small kitchen counter, and swept Laurie up in a big hug. He squeezed her close, swaying from side to side, and settled a long kiss on her waiting lips. Laurie sighed deeply when they finally parted.

"Busy today?" she asked.

"As always. Good thing I'm not claustrophobic. I spent two hours in a three-foot-high crawlspace this afternoon. How about you? Were you able to get some writing done?"

"A little," she said. At least it was an honest answer. She had gotten a little done, but would rectify that later. "What's for supper?"

Laurie rarely bothered to fix anything in her own apartment. In fact her pantry had little in it besides food bars and cold cereal. Chase's pantry, on the other hand, was well stocked with the staples, and if his spice rack had only the basics, well, at least he had a spice rack.

"I picked up this roasted chicken yesterday. I thought we'd make chicken salad with half of it, and throw the rest in the soup pot." As he spoke he dragged his soup pot out from under the counter, and found a bowl for the salad. "Want to take the meat off the bones while I take a shower?" He gave her his best puppy-dog look. "I'll be out in a minute," he said, and dashed off toward the bathroom.

Laurie started pulling the skin off the roasted chicken, chopping the breast meat on the cutting board and setting aside skin and bones to boil for soup stock. She didn't mind sharing the kitchen chores with Chase, only because she knew they were truly shared. Yesterday he had made shepherd's pie, and it was delicious.

Laurie heard the shower turn off, and Chase opened the bathroom door to let the steam out. She glanced up from her work to watch him towel dry. He was a sight she didn't get tired of. Lean and mus-cular, one might think he spent his days at the gym rather than running the busiest HVAC company in the county – one he would own, once he earned enough equity in the business. He wrapped a towel around his waist, came into the kitchen for a kiss, and snagged a piece of chicken, popping it into his mouth.

"We worked a job in Peach Valley today. Some beautiful houses over that way, and lots of pretty countryside, but still fairly close to town. We'll take a ride out there one of these days."

Chase headed to the bedroom for some clothes, and padded into the living room a moment later in bare feet, khaki shorts, and a forest green tee shirt. He selected a bossa nova channel from his favorite music streaming service – music was Chase's other passion – and his speaker came to life.

He returned to the kitchen, fingers snapping and hips swaying. He took Laurie by the wrists – she was holding a knife in one hand, and her other hand was shiny with chicken grease – and danced her around the living room in a vague imitation of a rumba. "This is exciting. I don't remember the last time I danced with a woman who was holding a large knife."

"Lucky for you music soothes the savage beast. Otherwise you might have found yourself in the soup pot."

He released her and the two returned to the kitchen. Chase chopped celery for the chicken salad, tossed it in the bowl with the chicken, and started adding mayonnaise.

"Easy on the mayo there, pal," Laurie said. "Hey, you'll never guess who I heard from today."

"You're probably right," Chase said, and ducked his head as Laurie reached for the knife again.

"So I'll tell you, smarty-pants. My brother Mike called. He's coming down from Dayton to Atlanta on business, and wants to make a side trip here to meet you. And see me, of course."

"That's nice. I thought you told me he never comes south."

"Well, this is some special convention or whatever that his company is sending him to. Anyway, Mike said he'll probably drive down, and I asked if he'd bring my things from the storage unit. I left all my winter clothes up there, and a few pieces of furniture and some books and things that I want."

"So you've decided to stay in Georgia, have you? I'm glad to hear that," Chase said. He meant it as a joke, but then added sincerely, "Very glad. So what will your brother do, get a U-Haul, or something?"

"Dad has a truck, and a small trailer. I'm sure Mike can borrow them. He's supposed to let me know. It's another few weeks before he's due to come down." Laurie paused, her knife in the air. "He said he ran into my ex the other day. And his new wife, that..." Laurie paused, searching for the right word, and settled on "hag."

"Tell us how you really feel," Chase said.

"It just torques me that he got married so fast. Two months after our divorce was final."

"Do you miss him?" Chase asked.

"God, no!" Laurie exclaimed. "Good riddance."

"Back to your brother's visit. How much stuff do you have? Will it fit in our two apartments?"

"Oh, some of it will, and the rest..." Laurie had a thoughtful expression on her face. "You know, when I see it all, I'll probably wonder why I kept a lot of it. I want my clothes and a few family mementos, but I'll probably take some stuff to the Treasure Chest."

The Treasure Chest, a thrift shop operated by St. Mark's, was Laurie's pet charity. She volunteered there whenever she had free time.

Laurie's phone dinged, and she pointed to it with a greasy finger. "See if that's Mike. Although I didn't expect to hear from him again tonight."

Chase grabbed her phone and read what was on the screen. "It's Mary. She says 'Guess what we got at TC today!!!!'" Chase pronounced the punctuation marks out loud, "Exclamation point, exclamation point, exclamation point, exclamation point."

Laurie snorted. "Probably some fabulous baby clothes."

"She gets that excited about baby clothes?"

"You have no idea. Although that is a lot of exclamation points, even for Mary. I'll text her after supper. Or, I'll probably see her at the shop tomorrow after work."

Mary was Laurie's best friend; the one who had talked her into moving south after her divorce from DB (a.k.a Dirt Bag). And Laurie had not regretted the move, especially after falling in love with Chase.

As they dug into their chicken salad Chase said, "I was going to get my guitar out after supper and work on a song or two. You want to bring your laptop down and write for a while?"

"Sure. I was planning to put some more time in." Laurie was used to working with noises around her, and once she got swept up in whatever she was writing, she wasn't easily distracted. For that matter, she really enjoyed the sound of Chase's guitar. It was a little like birdsong to her, a safe sound of "all's well."

After supper Chase cleared away the dishes and Laurie scampered up the stairs to her apartment to fetch her laptop. The two spent a companionable and productive evening together.

Finally Chase set his guitar down, stretched, and wandered to the kitchen for a drink of water. Then he stood behind Laurie as she tapped away on her laptop, and leaned down to wrap his arms around her shoulders.

"You're making it awfully hard to type," she said, tapping the keys more slowly.

"I thought it was time you worked on the steamy sex scene," he said.

"But..." She resisted half-heartedly as he nibbled at her neck.

"Consider it research. You know what they say: write what you know." He continued planting slow kisses on her collar bone and down her shoulder.

"But this novel didn't have a steamy .... Oh. Oh, well, maybe it does."

Chapter 2.

Laurie left her part-time job at the *Journal* Friday feeling good. She liked the freedom the job afforded, and especially enjoyed the creative aspects. Since starting there in the spring, she had managed to expand her duties – and pay – by quite a bit. Now she regularly provided feature articles for the newspaper, and had quite a few publishing credits to her name.

She drove the couple of blocks home, let herself into Chase's apartment, and made a sandwich of chicken salad leftover from the previous night. Then she filled her to-go cup with iced coffee and drove to the Treasure Chest.

The Treasure Chest was right next to St. Mark's. Both were across from the Tasty Chick restaurant, just north of downtown Chinkapin on the old Redding Road. The Treasure Chest sold a little bit of everything. All the items were donated by the community, and in turn the thrift shop supported other organizations in town with some of their proceeds.

Laurie had been volunteering there since the week she moved to Chinkapin.

The bells on the door jangled as Laurie breezed into the shop. "Hey, friends. How's it going?" Mary and Carol, another volunteer, were working in the office tagging clothes. They looked up and greeted her.

Laurie set her purse down on the desk in the office, and took a seat next to Mary as Carol went to wait on a customer. "How's Roly?" Laurie asked.

"*Ricky* is fine. And I'm fine too, thanks for asking."

Richard Leonard Roster was the infant's real name, but the first time Laurie heard it and pictured his monogram, RLR, it made her think of the word 'roller.' In her mind the baby would always be Roly. She couldn't resist cuddling her little godson whenever she got the chance. She wouldn't admit it to anyone, but she had more than a touch of baby fever.

"Who's watching him today?" she asked.

"Melissa, as usual. And I'll watch Brandon for her tomorrow. She and her husband want to test drive some cars. They really need something a little bigger since they have another child now."

Then Mary smiled impishly. "I picked out some more cute stuff today. Here, look." She held up a camouflage baby outfit, complete with little camo socks.

"No one in your family even hunts," Laurie protested.

"But it's so cute! And I have a great Elmer Fud hat at home. Look here." Mary pulled her phone out of her purse and showed Laurie the latest photos on Instagram.

"How many followers does he have now?" Laurie asked.

"Forty-eight." Mary tossed her head and smiled. She had a hard time not buying every cute baby item that came into the shop. She claimed she saved a lot of money that way. Laurie was not so sure.

Pretty much anything at the shop could be had for a bargain price, though. That was a problem occasionally, since every once in a while something was donated to the shop which just could not be sold for a song.

"Did you tell Laurie what happened yesterday?" Carol asked when the customer had gone.

"Oh!" Mary waved her hands and her eyes widened. "I forgot to tell you."

"What? Were we robbed again?" Laurie asked. One of the volunteers had been hit over the head during a robbery several months ago, but from the smile on Mary's face Laurie knew it was something good this time.

"You are not gonna believe this," Carol began.

"Oh, don't tell her! Don't tell her!" Mary cried. "I want to see her expression." She pulled open the bottom drawer of the file cabinet and handed Laurie a plastic bag.

"A book?" Laurie asked.

"Go on, look at it," Mary said. "Gently," she added as Laurie pulled it out of the bag.

Slowly Laurie turned it over. It was a gray, cloth bound book with royal blue writing on the cover. "Gone With the Wind. Margaret Mitchell," she read aloud. Then she opened it, and read "New York. The MacMillan Company. 1936. Is this a first edition?" She turned another page and gasped, eyes wide. "To Joseph Barnes. Margaret Mitchell. It's signed! By Margaret Mitchell. How cool is that?"

"A signed first edition! Can you believe it?" Mary pointed at the signature as Laurie examined it more closely. "It was in a box with some other books and a couple of old trophies."

"Who brought it in?"

Carol shook her head. "No one knows. The box was just left outside. They found it when they opened the shop yesterday."

"Well, this has to be worth something. Has Evelyn seen it?" Laurie asked. Evelyn always wanted to get every last penny out of anything that was donated to the shop. All in the name of supporting the church, Evelyn claimed.

"Not yet!" Mary said with a laugh. "But I was thinking the same thing you are. I don't know how to begin finding out what something like this is worth. Other than checking one of the big online retailers – the big 'A,' you know that river in South America, or Craig's Whatever, or something like that. Maybe Evelyn knows."

"I went to a museum once up in Atlanta that had all to do with Margaret Mitchell and *Gone With the Wind*," Carol said. "It was in a house where Margaret lived for a while. They had a display all about the movie premier and everything."

"As a future famous writer, I need to go check that out," Laurie said with a wink. "There's so much to see in Georgia. I need to take a road trip one of these days."

"You really do," Mary agreed. "You're a Georgia Peach, now. You have to get familiar with things around here."

The bells on the door jangled, and several customers came in together. The Treasure Chest was

holding its end-of-summer sale, so the shop remained fairly busy until closing time.

Shortly after four o'clock the women flipped the
sign on the door from 'open' to 'closed' and counted
the money in the till. "Woo-hoo!" Carol exclaimed.
"Look at this. We had a great day." She updated the
books and set aside the deposit.

"Can't beat that with a stick," Mary said. "I better
get home and relieve Melissa. Have you got exciting
plans for the weekend?" she asked Laurie.

"Not sure," Laurie said. "Chase was telling me
about some cool houses he saw in Peach Valley. Maybe we'll take a drive out there and do some explor-
ing."

Chapter 3.

"Aaaaaw," Laurie wailed, dropping her spoon which clattered against her soup plate. "I wanted to do something fun tomorrow. Why do you have to work?"

"I'm sorry," Chase said. They were eating supper in his apartment. "It's just a large, complicated, and time-sensitive project. We've had to fabricate some ducts, which we don't normally do, install new electrical components... Bottom line is, the kids will be back in school Monday, and the HVAC system needs to be running properly. It's going to take all hands tomorrow to get it done."

Laurie pouted.

"You could come to work with me. That might be fun," Chase suggested, smiling.

"Not on your life," she answered. She would have liked to collaborate with Chase on something, but definitely not one of his HVAC jobs. "Do you think it'll take all day?"

"I hope not. We'll be getting an early start. No one else wants to work all day Saturday either. Maybe we'll be able to get it done by lunch time. And then in the afternoon we can drive out to Peach Valley and I'll show you those houses I talked about."

"Well, I'm not getting up early to make you pancakes in the morning," Laurie said, sticking her nose in the air. "You'll just have to eat cold cereal."

* * *

Early the next morning Laurie pulled the covers over her head. She knew Chase was being as quiet as possible, but the light from the bathroom had awakened her. She heard the sound of him pulling on his work pants, and then the rattle of coins as he slid his loose change and his wallet into his pocket.

She softened a bit. She knew he didn't really want to go into work on Saturday either. He needed the business to be a success. His employees depended on it, and so did she and Chase. Laurie thought of the spreadsheet he had shown her, tracking the payments he was making to buy the business from his late wife's father. In less than six months Anderson HVAC would be his. Maybe even sooner, if they worked a lot of jobs.

She peeled the bedsheet away from one eye. Chase sat on the chair putting his shoes and socks on. He raised his head and caught her glance.

"You haven't changed your mind about those pancakes, have you?"

"Not a chance!" she said, pulling the sheet back over her head. "You may kiss me goodbye before you leave."

"I'll kiss you goodbye right now!" He growled, and dove onto the bed. She squealed as he planted a big kiss through the sheet where he imagined her forehead was.

"I'll let you know how things are going," he called, closing the bedroom door.

After fifteen minutes of trying to go back to sleep Laurie got up and contemplated her day. She slid her clothes on, trotted upstairs to her own apartment, and started the coffee brewing while she showered.

Several cups later Laurie had drafted a couple of hundred words in her latest opus, but could no longer ignore the complaints from her empty stomach. "Just because he's not here for breakfast doesn't mean I can't have a treat," she told herself. She packed up her laptop and headed to the Coffee Pot.

The Coffee Pot was the only café in Chinkapin, but even if it weren't Laurie knew it would still be her favorite. She loved everything about it: the coffee-themed décor, the retro furnishings, and especially the music of the '30's and '40's wafting from the sound system.

She also loved their cat-head biscuits. They were golden brown and slightly crispy on the outside, but fluffy, hot and delicious on the inside. She ordered one with egg and cheese, and a second that she could smear with butter and honey for dessert. She also ordered a large cup of her favorite latte, the Southern Classic. With several pumps of pecan syrup it tasted like a pecan pie. It was a feast fit for a queen. Maybe an empress.

The server brought the food to Laurie's table in the back of the café. Laurie snapped a picture and texted it to Chase. A moment later her phone dinged, and she read his reply.

You dirty dog!

She smiled and took a satisfied bite from a biscuit.

As she enjoyed her breakfast, she watched the other patrons, occasionally taking notes if she overheard an interesting comment or spotted an unusual-looking person. Laurie liked to people-watch. She didn't eavesdrop exactly, but she did keep her eyes and ears open for something she could use in a short story, or in the novel she had been working on for what seemed like forever. When fate handed her an interesting character, she liked to take advantage.

This morning a discussion group occupied the long table in the middle of the café. Other patrons, mostly couples or small groups, were scattered around. Laurie studied them to see if she knew any-one. A few did look vaguely familiar.

Since arriving in the spring, Laurie had immersed herself in activities and events around town, and had written newspaper articles about several of them. She had even hosted an art show at St. Mark's, and narrowly escaped getting involved with a local artist. *One man at a time, thank you very much*, she thought. She would limit her creative endeavors to writing from now on, and enjoy art from afar. She finished her second biscuit, and opened her laptop on the small table.

The café door opened and a man with a thick, curly, reddish beard and a rather interesting handle-bar mustache walked in. He was about the same height as Chase, maybe even taller, with a stocky build, and neatly dressed with a button-down shirt tucked into his slacks. Laurie supposed he might have come to the café from the courthouse across the street. She watched as he read the drinks menu posted above the counter. He ordered something, glanced around briefly, and then buried his nose in his cell phone.

Laurie studied him as he waited for his order. The man's curly hair reminded her a little of a Goldendoodle. And who knew when she'd need a character with a beard in one of her stories? She reached for her notebook to jot down a few lines about his appearance...and knocked over her latte.

Warm brown liquid streamed over the edge of the table and onto the floor. With a loud scrape she pushed back her chair and shoved her laptop out of the way. There was no chance of her clumsiness going unnoticed. All eyes were on Laurie. She bent with her napkin, partly to wipe up the spill, and partly in a futile attempt to hide her glowing cheeks. The server quickly appeared with a rag, and helped with the mopping up.

Laurie kept her head down as long as possible, and the other patrons soon lost interest. A moment later the barista handed a beverage to the man with the mustache, and he left the café.

Laurie ordered a second, smaller latte just to prove she hadn't been beaten, and spent another hour on her work. Finally she checked the time. *So much for Chase being done by lunch-time – or even letting me know how he's doing*, she thought.

A quick text elicited an apology. The job was taking longer than he had hoped. He'd just sent someone out to bring back burgers for the crew.

Laurie snapped her laptop shut. She was not in the mood to work anymore, and needed to stretch anyway. She left the café, loaded her things into the trunk of her car, and looked up and down Main Street.

It had gotten busier since she'd arrived at the café, and people strolled up and down the sidewalks. For a small town, Chinkapin had a surprisingly good selection of shops. There were antiques shops, clothing boutiques, a jewelry store, a bookstore, and an interior decorator's showroom, among others. Laurie had written articles about some of them, part of a series of articles profiling the owners and how they got started in business.

Oddly enough, she had never spent any time in the bookstore, Franklin's New and Used, catty corner across the street from the Coffee Pot. She had little room in her apartment to store books, so lately she'd just been buying ebooks. And like the other Treasure Chest volunteers, Laurie used the thrift shop as a lending library. She and her friends read the books that were donated to the shop, and then brought them back to sell.

She watched as a woman in pink and two children entered the store. Locking her car, Laurie crossed the street and went in after them.

Chapter 4.

The smell of old books instantly reminded Laurie of the library she frequented as a child. The children's section had a long, slant-top table with a little rail on it to hold the books up while kids read. She remembered being dropped off there with her sister and brother while her mom went upstairs to look at the grown-up's books.

She forced herself back to the present and looked around. The woman in pink was browsing in the craft books aisle, while the children investigated some toys and games.

Laurie glanced at the person working behind the checkout counter, and then did a double take. It was the man with the curly beard she had seen in the café. *Might as well get it over with*, she thought.

"Hi. I'm Laurie Lanton," she said, offering her hand, "the clumsy one from the Coffee Pot café. I saw you over there a little while ago."

"Luke Morgan," he said returning her handshake with a smile. Up close she decided he was a bit older than she'd thought at first, judging by the gray hairs which streaked his beard; mature, in an appealing, sexy kind of way. "They make a great cup of coffee there. Shame you wasted yours." She rolled her eyes. "I was just wishing I'd bought a large," he added.

"Your first time there, huh? I take it you're not from Chinkapin then," she said.

"Peach Valley," he explained. "I'm opening up a Franklin's bookstore there in a couple of months. Meanwhile, I'm getting a little on-the-job training here while the proprietor is on vacation."

"Oh, Franklin's is a chain?" Laurie said. "Tell me how the book exchange works. I'm confused. The sign says something about credits?"

Luke explained Franklin's policy. It involved giving credits for books traded in, which were redeemable for half off the price of any used book in the store.

"Does that include these?" Laurie pointed to some books in the glass case under the check-out counter. They looked antique, and were wrapped in protective packaging.

"Those are priced as marked. Milton, the owner, likes to scour estate sales, flea markets and such, and brings back really old books to sell. In fact, he and his wife are out on the hunt this weekend. That way their mini-vacation is also a tax write-off." He smiled, lifting his eyebrows. "Something I need to think about myself."

"So if one of his patrons brought in a rare book, or first edition, or something...?" Laurie asked.

"He'd probably look it over and quote them a price, but they might be better off selling it on their own. Or they could take it to the worm. That is, Bookworm up in Redding. They handle rare books, first editions, one-of-a-kind, and even take books like that on consignment. Again, for a percentage."

"Bookworm, huh?" Laurie said. The name made her smile. "I'll be in Redding next Saturday for my writers group, so I'll probably check them out."

"Are you a writer?" Luke asked, showing more in-terest.

"I do an occasional article for the *Journal,* and I also have a novel in the works." It was sometimes hard for Laurie to call herself a writer outright. If only she could get that novel finished.

"Me as well," Luke said.

"Oh, really! So what genre do you write? Or is it non-fiction?"

"I'm working on a thriller, actually my second in a series, although the first isn't published yet."

"I guess there won't be a problem getting your books into the Franklin's in Peach Valley," Laurie said smiling.

"Mwa-ha-ha." He gave his imitation of an evil laugh and twirled one end of his mustache. "That's part of my master plan. Plus, with running the store, I'll have a job until I make my first million through my novels." He flashed an engaging smile.

"I hear that," Laurie said. His smile had put Laurie on her guard. She had been a sucker once before for an engaging smile, and was sadder and wiser for it.

"Yeah, I'm partnering with a friend in Peach Valley to open the bookstore. She's providing the cash to get the franchise going, and I'm the cheap labor." He smiled again, this time a little sheepishly. He really did have an impressive beard, though. And Laurie guessed he must wax his mustache, to make it curve up the way it did at the ends. She liked the way his eyes crinkled when he smiled. She noticed they were brown, like Chase's.

"What's it like out in Peach Valley?" she asked. "I hear there are some beautiful old houses over that way."

"There are some nice areas, and some poorer ones. It's a little more blue-collar than Chinkapin, if you can believe that. There is quite a bit of manufacturing there. It's the county seat, though, so there's a courthouse. Also a university. I think the bookstore will be a great addition to the town. At least that's what I'm betting."

"So is there a writers group in Peach Valley?"

"No. I'm part of an online group, but I've been wanting to join a group that meets face to face."

Luke waited on a customer who had just brought a book to the counter, and Laurie wandered off to have a look around. The store had a good selection of popular fiction and young adult books, plus sections on travel, gardening, crafts, and other topics. She wasn't in the market for anything in particular.

When the customer had gone Laurie returned to the counter. "You should check out the Redding Writers. Maybe they can help you with your thriller. We meet once a month to critique each other's work and provide moral support. You can find the group on Facebook."

"Sounds good," he nodded. "Maybe I'll look into it."

"Nice meeting you. Great mustache, by the way." Laurie flipped him a thumbs-up. As she left the bookstore, she made a note to check out Bookworm the next time she was in Redding.

She checked her watch, returned to her car and drove to the Treasure Chest to help out until closing.

* * *

"I bought an almost-new waffle maker at the Treasure Chest today," Laurie said as she settled on the couch in Mary's living room. Chase was still working, and it was too early to start supper, so Laurie decided to pay a visit to her friend. "And you're going to have lots to look at next time you go in. They got some cute, cute, *cute* baby stuff donated today, just before closing."

"Ooh, I'll have to check it out," Mary said from the rocking chair where she held Ricky in her arms.

"How is my little friend? He doesn't usually nap this late, does he?"

"No. He was pretty fussy earlier today. I don't think he's feeling good." Gently she placed a hand on his forehead. "I'm getting hot holding him." She switched Ricky from one shoulder to the other.

"He does look a little flushed." Laurie looked around at the untidy living room. "You've let your standards slip, woman."

"Well, Pete's gone this weekend, and I just haven't been motivated to do a lot of housework."

"Me neither. Chase had to work this morning, which turned into all day. I really should go home and clean our two bathrooms before they're reclaimed by nature, but I'm just not feeling it."

Laurie felt a little sorry for Mary. She brought her something cool to drink, and tidied up the living room. "Well, I think I'll head to the apartment. Chase will be home eventually, I guess. Are you going to be okay?"

"Oh, sure. Hey, can you take Ricky for a minute while I run to the necessary room? I've been sitting so long I think my legs are asleep!"

The child whimpered as Laurie lifted him from Mary's arms. "Why don't we just put him in his crib?" she asked.

"Try it. Maybe he'll stay down this time."

Laurie put Ricky in his crib, and returned to the living room to wait for her friend. As soon as Mary came out of the bathroom, a whining started from the nursery.

Mary sighed, and her shoulders drooped. "Here we go again. That's what happened a while ago when I tried to put him down."

"Hmmm. Maybe it's his ears. Have you given him anything?" Laurie asked.

"Some of that baby stuff for fever." She looked at her watch. "I can't give him any more for a while."

"Well, girlfriend, I hate to leave you alone with a sick kid," Laurie said. "Call me if you need anything."

"Thanks. We'll be all right." Mary waved, and headed down the hall to the nursery as Laurie let herself out.

Chapter 5.

Sunday morning Laurie climbed the stairs to the choir loft and found her seat while Chase went to adjust the sound system. The chair next to Laurie's was empty, so she texted Mary.

Hey - how's Roly? You coming to church today?

Steve led the choir through vocal warm-ups, and they ran through all of the day's hymns before Laurie got a text back.

Staying home. He fussed all night

Laurie texted again.

Let me know if you need anything

"Mary's baby is sick," Laurie told Steve. "She won't be coming this morning."

Tracy, one of the sopranos, turned toward Laurie and nodded. "There's something going around. Ever since school started back, the kids have been passing around germs." Laurie nodded. She knew Ricky's babysitter Melissa had an older child in pre-K, so that meant Ricky was getting exposed to all kinds of things.

Chase finished setting up the sound system, and carried a clip-on microphone to Mother Barbara in the narthex. He took his seat in the choir in time to go through the anthem with the others. Laurie did her best on the alto part, but missed having Mary singing in her ear.

Honestly, she would rather have just listened, especially with Chase behind her. She never got tired of hearing him sing. And he was so talented at composing! She wished he had more time to work on his music, but like her, he had to earn a living.

"Do we need to go over that alto part, Laurie?" Steve asked, snapping her out of her reverie.

"No. Um, yes, please. Can I just hear the last page?" This time Laurie paid attention.

She managed to stay focused throughout the service, and particularly liked the morning's second reading, a passage from the second letter of James:

Finders Keepers

*If a brother or sister is naked and lacks daily food,
and one of you says to them, 'Go in peace; keep
warm and eat your fill,' and yet you do not supply
their bodily needs, what is the good of that? So
faith by itself, if it has no works, is dead.*

Mother Barbara centered her homily on the reading. Laurie glanced down from the choir loft with a smug smile, and looked for her friends who worked at the Treasure Chest with her. After all, didn't they help clothe the poor?

Then she shrank back. *A little humility might suit you once in a while*, she thought. She knew inside that one of the reasons she spent so much time working at the thrift shop was to keep from having to go home to an empty apartment.

After the service the choir spent several minutes going through their anthem for the following Sunday. When they came down from the loft, Mother Barbara cornered Laurie in the narthex. "Laurie, can I borrow you for a moment in my office? I'd like your help with some publicity for the Blessing of the Pets."

Laurie opened her eyes wide, and followed the priest to her office. "Okay, I'm all ears. What the heck is a blessing of the pets? I don't think I've run across that in the prayer book. Is that really a thing?"

"It's the way we honor the feast day of St. Francis of Assisi. You know, he considered all creatures – birds, animals, what have you – to be his brothers and sisters. He died on October 4, 1226, and for his feast day we have a special blessing of the animals. In our parish, there aren't any farm animals to speak of, unless you count the chickens a few of our members raise, so it translates into a blessing of the pets."

"I love the fresh eggs Amy brings in sometimes," Laurie said. "Especially the pretty green ones!"

"Yes, they are lovely. So, as I was saying, I was looking at my calendar earlier, and the Sunday closest to the fourth is...."

Laurie interrupted her. "Wait, people bring their pets to the morning service?"

Barbara looked at Laurie and rolled her eyes. "We hold the blessing in the afternoon. And outdoors too, of course." She pointed to the date on the calendar. "This is the date we're looking at. I don't expect many people from outside our parish to attend, but we might get a few interested enough to come and see what's going on. Will there be enough time to get an announcement in the newspaper?"

"Oh, yeah. I'll have no problem getting this into the events column. Now let me ask you a question," Laurie said. "Since this is all focused on pets, how come we don't try to have the animal shelter involved?" Earlier in the year St. Mark's had hosted an art show to benefit the shelter.

Mother Barbara just looked at her.

"I mean, our art show was such a success a few months ago. We got some good press from that. And you like to at least keep the community aware that there is an Episcopal church in town." She paused. "Are we the only church doing this pet blessing, do you think?"

"We are here in Chinkapin, yes. Truthfully, I'd like to cancel the whole thing, but there are members of the parish who would run me out on a rail if I did. They love their pets, and they enjoy seeing everyone else's."

"Then why would you want to cancel? It sounds like fun, actually."

Barbara sighed. "Anything can happen where animals are concerned. I officiated at a wedding one time – an outdoor wedding – where the bride insisted that a pair of doves be released at the end of the ceremony. Well, the man with the birdcage opened it, but the doves wouldn't come out. So, he reached into the cage and tossed them into the air. No sooner did they flutter up into the lovely blue sky than a hawk swooped down, seized one of them, and carried it off."

"No way!" Laurie's mouth dropped open.

"And the wedding guests kept asking *me* whose bird I thought got eaten, the groom's or the bride's, and whether it was some kind of a bad omen. They did end up getting divorced, come to think of it." Mother Barbara smiled at the memory, in spite of the divorce. "Ah, well. Sometimes I think divorce is proof that God wants us to be happy."

"Amen to that!" Laurie said.

"And, of course, not all pets play well with others. When some of them get nervous or excited their little bodies react in strange and wonderful ways. Which reminds me to make sure this year we have plenty of baggies on hand to pick up doggy waste." Barbara jotted a note as she talked.

The little wheels were still turning in Laurie's head. "It still seems like a no-brainer to maybe host a pet adoption or something. As you said, most animal lovers I know like to see other pets. And if we do get people from outside the parish who are just there to check out the event and see the fun, that'll be more for them to look at. Who knows, maybe they'll decide to adopt a pet."

Laurie was surprised when Mother Barbara didn't jump all over the idea. "Well," she said, "the service itself is not terribly long. Plus, people usually have their hands full if they've brought their own animals. And you're assuming the animal shelter will be on board with this. They'd have to already have pets that they deemed adoptable, and a way to transport them to the church. We don't really have a lot of time to plan this."

Laurie pouted, and finally Barbara said, "But, far be it from me to stop someone from bringing people to the church. You have my permission to make inquiries at the animal shelter. Let me know what they say, and I'll run it by the vestry."

"Yay," Laurie said, clapping her hands. She knew just who she needed to talk to, and made a note to call the Chinkapin animal shelter first thing Monday.

Chapter 6.

Laurie found Chase chatting with Steve the organist in the parish hall. Chase downed the last swallow from his coffee cup just as Laurie made a grab for it. "Waah! No coffee left!"

"I need to buy some guitar strings. Want to run up to Redding?" Chase asked. "We can find a place for brunch and coffee up there."

"Yay! I'd like to go to Redding. In fact, there's a bookstore I heard about recently that I wanted to find."

"What's it called?" Chase asked, as Laurie took out her phone and started to look up the address.

"Book-something."

Chase laughed.

"Bookworm. That was it. How could I forget? The guy who told me about it called it 'the worm.'" She scrolled for a minute. "Here it is. But, never mind. It's closed on Sundays. Oh, well. Let's go find some-place for breakfast. I'm starved!"

Laurie liked Redding. A college town, it was big enough and artsy enough to be interesting, but not so sprawling or crowded that it was hard to get around. Chase drove the "scenic route" – what they called any route that didn't involve the interstate – and soon Laurie was drinking coffee and enjoying a thick slice of avocado toast in an old diner-style restaurant while Chase plowed his way through an omelet and fried potatoes.

In the music store, Laurie waited patiently as Chase checked out a guitar. He wasn't really in the market for a new one, but liked to see what he was missing every once in a while. "This one's a beauty. Listen," he said, strumming some chords, sliding his fingers up and down the fret board.

"If you say so." Laurie smiled, not really sure what she was listening for.

She looked at the keyboards and poked a few keys. She was mildly interested in picking up music lessons again, and knew Steve could give her piano lessons. But she wasn't interested enough to pay what a keyboard cost, and didn't have much room for one in her apartment. But maybe someday.

Finally Chase paid for the strings he needed and they returned to their car. "Now what?" he asked.

"Let's ride through some of the old neighbor-hoods in town, just to check them out," she said.

He clicked the fob to unlock the car doors. "Hop in. I'd like to look at that area near the university."

A few minutes later Chase cruised slowly down a street full of two-story houses with neat porches and narrow yards. "Some of these are nice."

Laurie saw a couple of young female students in short-shorts walking toward the park that served as a front yard for the university. "Not exactly what I was hoping for," she said, glancing at Chase to see if he had noticed too. "Maybe a bit more yard? I know: let's drive over toward Riverview. I hear it's the up-and-coming neighborhood in town."

"Hmm," Chase said, negotiating his way down an alley. "I don't think it's come up as much as you think. It's still a rather rough area, according to the newspapers."

"And it'll stay rough if nice people run away from it all the time. I think it's a great location. It has good access to the freeway, but not too close. And it's near downtown, and the hospital, and also near the old riverfront park."

"It does have a few things going for it." Chase cut through town and was soon driving up and down res-idential streets.

"Ooh, look at that wrap-around porch!" Laurie pointed.

"And boarded-up windows."

"The one across the street is fixed up," she said hopefully.

"I thought you wanted more yard, though."

Laurie slouched in her seat as Chase turned a corner and headed down another street.

"Oh! Stop! Stop!" Laurie sat up straight and pointed through the windshield.

Chase rolled to a stop, checking his rearview mirror to be sure there was no one behind him. "Which one?" he asked.

"This one right here! On the corner! Look how nice and big the yard is. And flat too, not a million steps leading to the front porch."

"More boarded up windows. But the porch isn't bad," Chase said.

"Mostly one story, I guess, but look at that dormer above the porch. Maybe an attic, or one big room up there? I wish we could see inside."

"I wish we could too," Chase said, a little less enthusiastically. He drove past several lots and turned around in a driveway, then drove slowly past the house again and turned at the corner so they could see the side of it. "It's pretty large, actually. Sort of L-shaped."

"That must be the kitchen, there in the back. And what's this little building? Do you think it goes with the main house?" She indicated a small structure at the back of the lot that wasn't visible from the front. It looked like a small house, with a tiny porch, and a chimney hinting at a fireplace inside. "How cute that looks! That could be my little writing retreat!"

"Or my music studio," Chase said.

"I claimed it first!"

"Okay, then, you can kill all the roaches and mice that probably live in there."

"Killjoy," Laurie said, slugging him on the arm. "Turn around again. Let's see if there's an address." Chase turned the car around as Laurie noted the street sign on the corner.

"Well, some of these houses are lived in and look pretty well cared-for, but others...." Chase shook his head.

"They just need some love. Oh, wouldn't it be fun to work on a house like this together? You should have seen the house they rehabbed on HGTV the other day. Ten times worse than this."

"The one that needed the surprise foundation work, to the tune of $30k?"

"It wasn't $30k, and you know they have to have a crisis in those shows. Remember the one where the crisis was 'Oh, no! We need to install Ground Fault Interrupt electrical outlets in the kitchen! What will the homeowners say??'" Laurie craned her neck to see around Chase. "Seriously, I like this house. And it's vacant."

"More like abandoned," Chase said under his breath. But Laurie gazed over her shoulder until the house was out of sight.

Chapter 7.

Monday morning as soon as Laurie got to work she placed a call to Glenda at the Chinkapin animal shelter. As Laurie expected, Glenda was all in favor of an adoption event, and confirmed that they would be free on the date of the blessing. She knew just the pets she wanted to bring along. She even contributed some ideas of her own to add a little more pizazz to the event. Laurie was delighted. She passed the info along to Mother Barbara, and wrote up the announcement for the newspaper.

She checked her watch a few times and finally decided it was late enough in the morning to call Mary.

"How's my little godson today. Any better?"

"Can you believe I broke down and took him to the urgent care last night?" Mary told her. "Ricky has an ear infection, and they put him on some antibiotics. I sure hope the meds don't tear his stomach up."

"An ear infection, huh? I remember those days, with my little brother," Laurie sympathized. "What happened to that immunity he was supposed to get from breastfeeding?"

"In case you hadn't noticed, I haven't been feeding him near as much, and haven't been pumping. He's been getting over half formula. I just couldn't sit there with him latched on for hours. But enough about my boobs. Did you guys do anything fun yesterday?"

"Chase wanted to go to the music store up in Redding," Laurie said. "And we went to a quirky little diner for brunch. It was short on décor, but the avocado toast sure was good. Then we drove around some of the older neighborhoods for a while. There are some beautiful houses up there."

"And some scary ones, I'll bet."

"Where's your sense of adventure? I think it would be fun to rehab an old house."

"Fun if you like working your ass off and going broke in the process. Fun if you want to spend every night and weekend working on the house, and never going anywhere."

"Did you hear that?" Laurie said. "I just stuck my tongue out at you. But hey, I took some pictures of the house I liked. I can show you, if you want to meet for lunch."

"I'm going to stay close to home until Ricky feels better. I'm waiting for that antibiotic to kick in. He's still running a fever."

"Okay. I'll check on you later. And if you need anything, just call me."

* * *

"I'm sure glad you could come in to help out today," Carol said as Laurie set her purse down in the Treasure Chest office and plopped into a chair. It was Tuesday, and Carol had called Laurie at the *Journal* to see if she was free that afternoon.

"So what happened to Alice?" Laurie asked.

"You just missed her. Don came by and picked her up. Bless her heart, she was confused about the date, and didn't realize today was her doctor's appointment."

"Well, I wanted to come talk to you anyway," Laurie said. "Since you're a real-estate guru, I was hoping you could help me find out some info about a house I'm interested in up in Redding."

"In Redding!" Carol said. "That's quite a commute from here!"

"Yeah, but there are some beautiful historic houses up there. Chase and I drove around to look at a few neighborhoods Sunday. Take a look at this." Laurie scrolled through the photos on her phone, and handed it to Carol.

"Hmmm. Nice yard. And boarded up windows. Looks like it needs some work. Now where exactly is it?"

"Over in Riverview."

"Riverview! Lord, you do like a challenge."

Once again, Laurie ran through all the reasons she thought the Riverview neighborhood was on the brink of a renaissance.

"And you wanted me to find out what?" Carol asked.

"Well, who the owner is, and what it's worth. I mean, it looks empty, so I'm just guessing whoever owns it would be willing to sell. Plus, did you look at this picture here?" Laurie scrolled to one showing the small building in the back yard, and handed Carol the phone again. "I was hoping to find out if this goes with the main house."

Carol looked at the picture. "Hmmm. Well, here." She clicked away on Laurie's phone. "This is the tax assessor's website. Keeping in mind it's a lot easier to see everything on a bigger screen. Now what's the address?" Laurie told her, and Carol tapped and scrolled until she found what she was looking for. "And there it is."

Laurie squinted at the small image on the phone. "That's the one. Are there more pictures?"

"Sure." Carol took the phone again and Laurie looked over her shoulder. "See there. That's a satellite image, with the lot line drawn over it. And there's your little building in the back yard, so it is included." She scrolled a bit more. "And look here. Here's the description of the buildings."

Laurie took her phone back and read the description aloud, interjecting comments. "Well, it's not quite a hundred years old, but almost. And the little building in the back is newer. I'm surprised at that. I thought maybe that was the original cabin or something, and then they built the big house in front." She read some more to herself. "So according to the tax assessor, the whole thing is only worth thirty thousand dollars!"

"That doesn't mean the owner will part with it for that, though. Plus you still don't know if the owner is even willing to sell."

"Camille Willingham, you mean. That's who's listed as the owner. So what do I do, send her a letter? Her address is here."

"If you're serious, your best bet is to work with a realtor. They'd probably help keep you out of trouble, plus the owner is more likely to respond to a realtor than to Joe Schmoe off the street. The realtor should be able to find out more about the history of the house – whether it ever flooded, or anything like that. Being that close to the river, you never know. And based on the pictures, the place has been rode hard and put up wet."

Laurie's virtual house hunt was interrupted, and she and Carol spent the rest of the afternoon waiting on customers, visiting with friends who stopped by, and cleaning up donated items to sell.

At four o'clock Laurie walked through the shop turning off lights while Carol tallied up the sales and counted the money in the cash drawer. "Right on the money," Carol said with a final jab at the calculator. "I love it when everything comes out even. We let Alice work the register last week. Lord, that was a mistake. We about never got the money straightened out." She set aside the deposit and updated the book where they tracked their daily totals. "Poor Alice, bless her heart. I worry about her when she leaves here sometimes, whether she'll make it home or get lost along the way. I wish Don would drop her off and pick her up all the time, but she won't hardly let him."

Laurie looked at her in some surprise. "Alice has always been a bit scatter-brained, hasn't she?"

"Well, but she's getting worse lately." Carol sighed, and gathered the deposit and her purse, shaking her head. "Are you staying here all night, Laurie?"

Laurie preceded Carol out of the shop and waited while her friend locked the door. She was still thinking about Alice, and pondering what she knew – which she realized was not much at all. Her husband Don seemed mighty protective of her. Laurie had always thought that was sweet, bordering on controlling, although Alice never seemed to mind. Now she wondered if Don had other reasons for keeping such a careful eye on his wife.

Chapter 8.

Laurie's thoughts of Alice were replaced by thoughts of what she and Chase would have for dinner. She texted him to find out whether he had plans. When he didn't reply right away she drove the short distance to her apartment.

By the time she pulled into a parking space, Chase had answered that he was staying at the jobsite until the work was done. It might take a couple more hours, but he hoped it would mean they wouldn't have to return there the next day.

Laurie groaned when she read the message. Then she tossed her phone into her purse and sat in the car with her arms folded. It looked like Chase was turning into a workaholic. She had hoped she'd left that behind after the divorce. She remembered all of DB's late nights "on the job," which turned out to be late nights playing the field, or out with that witch with a capital B.

She trudged up the stairs to her apartment, kicked off her shoes, and sat at her desk staring at her laptop. She had been on a roll working on her novel the previous afternoon. Maybe she could get back into it. She set the timer on her phone to remind her to get up and stretch. Otherwise she'd sit at the computer until her joints stiffened and her shoulders ached. Heaven knew she was already broad enough in the hip. She needed to get more exercise. Holding the counter up at the Treasure Chest just wasn't doing it.

Laurie typed away until the timer went off. Then she trotted down to the ground floor and let herself into Chase's apartment. She pulled a package of half-frozen steak out of the fridge and put it on the counter to thaw. Then she locked up again and took a short walk up the street, still thinking about her writing project, and wondering just how much bad news to throw at her main characters.

She intended to walk to the corner, but turned around a hundred yards short and fairly flew back to her apartment building and up the stairs. Her hands hit the keyboard before her bottom hit the chair – the inspiration was just that good.

Finally, her brainstorm safely stored in bits and bytes in her laptop, she rolled her shoulders, checked the time on her phone, and went back down the stairs. She found Chase at his door, just letting himself in. He greeted her with a tired peck on the lips. "I'm filthy. Let me jump in the shower."

He opened the door and looked around. "Are we eating up in your place tonight?"

Laurie looked blankly at him. "Well, no. I was hoping you'd grill these steaks, if they're thawed." A little charcoal grill and a dilapidated picnic table on a strip of worn grass were the only amenities their apartment complex boasted.

Chase poked at the meat in the package. The edges were thawed, but the middle still felt hard. From the slump of his shoulders she realized that grilling wasn't such a hot idea. "I was hoping you'd have something fixed already. I'm starving." He leaned back against the door.

"Well, sorry," Laurie said, feeling irritated. "If you would have texted me your order...." She looked him over. He was filthy, and sweaty, and his tee shirt was ripped. "I thought you weren't going to have to go out on jobs any more. Aren't you supposed to be the boss?"

He breathed an exasperated sigh. "I will be the boss, when I finally pay off the Old Man, as you well know. And I can pay him off more quickly if we take on more jobs and I do some of the labor myself. I've got to take the jobs when they come in. I can't schedule when people's heating and cooling systems are going to break down."

"Sorry," Laurie said. She knew it would be a while longer before Chase had finished buying out the business from "Old Man" Anderson. And Chase was working hard at it, in order to be debt-free so he and Laurie could get on with their lives, get a house together, and get married – or so Laurie hoped.

"Never mind," Chase said. "Look, I'll just run over to the Chick and get something. Do you want anything?"

"No," Laurie said. She loved the chicken tenders from the Tasty Chick, the restaurant across from St. Mark's. But she really did try to watch what she ate, and she really didn't need another meal of fried food.

"I'll see you in a bit, then," Chase said and left, closing the door behind him.

Laurie stared at the inside of the door. "What am I supposed to eat?" she asked aloud. She had just realized how hungry she was.

She poked at the package of steaks, then tossed them back in the fridge, and left Chase's apartment for her own.

Laurie ate her peanut butter sandwich and grumbled. What did Chase think she was, a short-order cook? One of the things she had always appreciated about him was his willingness to pitch in with cooking, and how good he was at it. But lately he'd been so busy that either she was eating alone, or they were going out, or she was doing the cooking herself. Was that what her future held for her? If that was it, then no thank you. She had been there and done that.

She stared at her phone, debating whether to call him. Instead, she worked on her manicure.

Nearly an hour later, her phone finally rang. She read Chase's name on the display, and hesitated before answering.

"Hey," he said. "Are you coming down?"

"Oh, I'm fine, thanks, and how are you?" Laurie answered sulkily. Apparently whether she'd had anything for supper or not wasn't too high on Chase's list of worries.

"Look, I'm sorry. I was just really tired when I came home. The day got away from me. Hopefully things will slow down as the season winds down."

"Hopefully," Laurie agreed. There was silence. "I'm just going to stay up here tonight. I've had a long day too. We're both tired. I'll see you tomorrow." Laurie was surprised to hear the words coming out of her mouth.

There was silence on the phone, and Laurie looked at the display to see if she had been cut off.

Then she heard Chase's voice again. "Sure. Probably a good idea. I'll talk to you tomorrow."

"Talk to you tomorrow. 'Bye." She stared at her phone. After a long pause, the little phone icon winked out. *He didn't even say "I love you,"* she thought.

Chapter 9.

Wednesday morning was slow at the *Journal*. Laurie made short work of rewriting the few events that had been submitted for the events column. She tried to follow up on a couple which sounded like they might turn into feature stories, including a notice about the upcoming production at the little theater. Unfortunately, early morning was not the best time to reach someone who spent late nights at rehearsals. Finally Laurie gave up, and tried to look busy as she surfed the web and thought about the previous night.

Chase seemed a bit moody lately, and Laurie wondered if it was more than just the long hours at work. Could it have something to do with his late wife's death – an anniversary, or something? Laurie had never asked when Jenny died. With a shock it occurred to her that Jenny's grave must be in Chinkapin somewhere. After all, her family was from Chinkapin, which was how Chase had wound up here.

She tossed out a nasty cup of coffee that had steeped too long in the communal coffee pot, and called it quits. She craved her favorite latte and decided to go to the café.

"Your usual?" The young woman at the Coffee Pot greeted Laurie with a smile. Laurie regretted that she still couldn't remember her name.

"Yeah, a southern classic, hot. Make it with soy this time." No matter how many other flavors she tried, Laurie always came back to the same one. Maybe she was turning into a southerner after all. "And how about a turkey and gouda on whole grain? Tomato, no lettuce."

She sat at a small table near the back. She would have preferred one against the wall, but left those for larger parties. It was lunchtime, and the café was filling up fast. She guessed there must be something going on at the courthouse across the street, for the place to be this full.

While she waited for her lunch, Laurie called Mary to find out how her little godson was doing. No one answered, so she left a message.

She resisted the urge to call Chase – usually they talked to each other around lunchtime – but she couldn't stop thinking about him. Hopefully he would be through with work at a decent hour today, and be able to spend some time with her in the evening. She felt a twinge of worry, wondering if he was working through lunch. She hated skipping meals. Once she felt hungry she couldn't concentrate on anything but food.

She was glad when the server brought her sandwich and coffee. She took the lid off the latte to let it cool, and shoved the unwanted dill pickle spear to the side, hoping the juice hadn't sopped into her sandwich.

A man's voice above her said, "Nasty things, dill pickles."

Laurie raised her head, startled. Right away she recognized the distinctive beard and handlebar mustache. A moment later her brain came up with his name. "Luke! Hi." She paused, registering what he had said. "Yeah, dill pickles. They're usually too sour for me. One of these days I'll remember to ask them to leave it off my plate."

Luke stood above her smiling, making Laurie feel awkward. "So...have you ordered? Would you like to join...?" She gestured toward the seat across from her at the table.

"Thanks," he said, "but I just have time to grab a coffee and run back across the street. More OJT at Franklin's."

"Gotcha. So when will your shop open, again?" Suddenly Laurie was in reporter mode. Her senses detected a story, possibly for the *Journal*, but definitely for its sister publication, the *Register*, which covered news in the county where Peach Valley was located. She'd have to find out whether an article about the store had been written yet.

"Three weeks. It's coming up fast. Construction is done, shelves are up, and we'll be getting a shipment of books in another week. Until then, it's hurry up and wait."

The server called Luke's name, and he grabbed his coffee, waved, and left. *Oh, well,* Laurie thought. *I can run across after lunch and ask about writing that article.* She took a big bite of her sandwich, and her phone rang. Mary's name popped up. She wiped her fingers on a napkin, swiped across the screen and said a muffled "Hello, Mary."

"You sound like you're eating."

Laurie took a moment, and finally swallowed. "The universe must think I need to go on a diet. My lunch keeps getting interrupted. I'm glad you called, though. How's Roly?"

Over the phone Laurie heard a big sigh. "Not good. He still doesn't seem to be getting any better. I mean, not considering he's been on anti-biotics for a couple of days now."

"I'm sorry to hear that. Have you called the doctor?"

"Yes. They said to bring him in tomorrow if he's not any better. I wish I'd taken him in this morning. If I go now, I know their office will be slammed. But I can tell something's just not right."

"Listen, maybe I'll drop over for a bit after I eat."

"That would be great," Mary said. "I'd enjoy seeing another adult."

Chapter 10.

Mary answered her door wearing a pair of jean shorts, a Georgia Bulldogs tee shirt, and shiny gold slippers with ivory pom-poms on top. Ricky was on her hip, looking pinker than usual.

"Love the slippers," Laurie said smiling.

"Are these not just the cutest? My sister found them in a thrift shop and sent them to me. They came today. The rest of me is a mess, but at least my feet are gorgeous."

Laurie followed Mary inside and took the baby from her arms. "How's my little Roly?" she said addressing him. "Your forehead feels warm. Tell momma to turn on some air conditioning!"

"I just took his temp and gave him some more medicine. Want something to drink?" Mary led the way to the kitchen.

"Just some water with a little ice, please." Laurie sat at the breakfast table with Ricky on her lap and looked around at the cluttered kitchen.

"I'm going kind-of stir crazy today. I took a walk early this morning while Pete was watching the baby. He went in late to work. I hope that doesn't mean he has to stay until seven o'clock tonight." She brought a couple of glasses to the table, and sat opposite Laurie. She picked up her phone from the kitchen table, propped her feet up on the edge of the seat next to her, and snapped a photo.

"Why are you taking a picture of your feet?" Laurie asked.

"I'm putting this on Instagram to show my sister the slippers she sent."

Laurie rolled her eyes. "You are going stir crazy."

"Hey, I'll have you know we have thirty more followers. Ricky's pictures always get the most likes, though. I've been posting cute pictures of him in his thrift shop threads." She was suddenly thoughtful. "Hey, 'thrift shop threads.' I like the sound of that." Finally she put down her phone and got up to putter around the kitchen. "So how's your week going?"

"Oh. You know. Slow at work today." Laurie swirled the ice around in her glass. "And Chase has been really busy lately. I hardly saw him yesterday."

"I know how that is. It's hard to find the right balance between a guy who works too much and one who doesn't work at all. And you want them to be around when you want them around, but not under-foot. I'm just glad Pete's not on the road this week, because I can't get a thing done with Ricky feeling bad and wanting to be held all the time."

Laurie nodded, cradling Ricky in her lap. He sat with his back leaned against her. "Mary, is he wheez-ing?" she asked. "Poor guy, he just seems droopy to-day. Not his usual happy self."

"He's *not* his usual self." She had fixed him a small bottle, and held it out to him. Ricky reached for it, so Mary took the baby back in her arms, sat opposite Laurie and gave him the bottle. "At least he still has an appetite." The baby settled in Mary's arms, slowly nursing. "I haven't had a chance to do any of my usual chores. And I really need to get out to the grocery store."

"I'll be glad to run to the store for you," Laurie said. She wasn't really *glad* glad. She certainly didn't take delight in grocery shopping. But she felt it was the type of thing she ought to say, if she was going to love her neighbor like Mother Barbara had talked about in her last sermon.

"Would you? Oh, great. Here, I was making a list." Mary got up awkwardly, balancing the still-nursing Ricky. One-handedly she tore a slip of paper off a small pad on the kitchen counter.

Laurie looked it over. There was a lot of stuff on the list, but she *had* volunteered, so she couldn't back out now. "I'll go get this stuff while Roly's eating," she said.

A short while later she wheeled her cart around the grocery store – her 'buggy' in the local vernacular, as Laurie reminded herself – and pondered the turn Mary's life had taken since she'd had the baby. Normally very particular about her home, she now had little time for housework. Laurie used to endure lectures from Mary about all the things she 'should' do – clean up or decorate her apartment, update her wardrobe, and on and on. Today there were dishes in Mary's sink and unfolded laundry on the living room couch.

She turned a corner to go down another aisle, and found her way blocked by a man walking with a cane and a woman following behind him in an electric grocery cart. The woman must have heard Laurie's heavy sigh. She half-turned and peered at Laurie out of the corner of her eye. "Arthur, I think we're in the way," she called to her husband. "Arthur!" she said again sharply. "We're in the way."

Arthur was stooped over, head tilted back, squinting through his bifocals at items on the bottom shelf. He straightened slowly and shuffled up the aisle a few paces so his wife had room to move her cart aside. "Sorry about that," the woman said.

Laurie regretted her impatience. "No problem." A bit louder, she said to Arthur, "Can I help you find something?"

"Yeah," he said. "My lost youth!" There was a twinkle in his eye.

Laurie laughed, shaking her head. "Try Kroger's. They sometimes have a better selection." She smiled at the couple, and moved on down the aisle, telling herself, *patience, Laurie. Patience.*

A moment later she stood in the baby-food aisle pondering the mysteries of infant formula. She never realized how many kinds and sizes there were. She found what she was looking for, but lingered to admire the cute packaging on all the baby items.

She wasn't at all worried about her biological clock. Was she? Lots of women much older than Laurie had babies every day. She sure didn't feel ready to go through what Mary was going through.

But something happened to Laurie when she held Roly. He was so soft and sweet, and just felt good in her arms. *Patience, Laurie, Patience*, she reminded herself. *Let's not put the cart before the horse.* Having a baby was a two-person operation, and she was still single.

She was still single, she had spent the night alone, and she hadn't heard from her boyfriend all day.

Laurie wasn't sure she had the patience for a husband, let alone a baby. Especially when she was still trying to get her career off the ground.

She made it through the check-out line, returned to Mary's house, and schlepped the grocery bags in. Mary joined her in the kitchen, still holding Ricky. "I was hoping he'd take a nap after that bottle, so I could take a shower. But whenever I try to put him down... I guess his ears still hurt."

Laurie listened as she emptied the bags and put a few things in the refrigerator. "I really appreciate you doing this," Mary said swaying back and forth with the baby on her hip. "Was the store crowded?"

Laurie let out a laugh. "It's senior discount day, so I had to dodge a few electric carts. They should make those people take a driver's test." She finished unpacking, and looked at her friend. "Mary, you look pathetic. Or as they say in the South, 'Shuguh, wouldn't you feel bettuh with a little lipstick on?'"

The two burst out laughing, but Laurie could see tears in Mary's eyes. "Seriously, hand that baby to me and go take a shower before Pete gets home."

Mary didn't have to be told twice. She gently transferred Ricky into Laurie's arms and dashed down the hall. Laurie carried the baby into the living room and sat with him in the recliner. He studied her a moment wide-eyed and then grabbed a lock of her brown hair.

She tried in vain to unwind it from his fist, and then gave up. "How about a story, little one? It's about a girl named Goldilocks. Stop me if you've heard it before." She droned on with the drumming of the shower in the background, and was startled when Pete walked into the living room.

"Hi!" he said, as surprised as Laurie was. "How are you?" Ricky reached for him, so Pete lifted him from Laurie's lap.

"I'm fine. I'm afraid Roly's still not feeling very well. He won't let us lay him down. I sent Mary off to take a shower. Why don't you two run out for a quick supper, just so she can get out of the house? I can watch him for another hour or so."

"That sounds like a good idea. Let me go see how Mary's doing."

A minute later the three of them came out into the living room. Mary looked refreshed. Her wet hair was pulled into a neat bun, and she had some blush and a swipe of lipstick on. "Pete said you offered to watch Ricky while we run out for a bite? Just over to the little Mexican restaurant up the road."

"Sure. Take your time. Roly and I will be just fine." Pete handed the baby back to her as Laurie pulled the lever to pop up the recliner's footrest. "Just bring my purse over here so I'll have my phone handy."

Mary gathered her purse and cell phone, and pulled a light jacket out of the closet, all the while glancing back at Ricky. "If he seems hungry...."

Laurie cut her off. "I know where everything is. Just go! I'll call you if anything happens."

Pete took Mary by the elbow and steered her toward the garage. "See you later," he called.

Laurie heard the car pull away, and the garage door close with a groan. "It's just you and me, kid," she said to Ricky. "Don't start crying now, or fill your diaper or anything." The baby looked solemn, and then settled into her arms, his head against her chest.

Laurie fished her phone from her purse next to her and called Chase's number. He answered on the second ring.

"Hey. You coming down? I reworked my schedule so we could spend some time together this evening. I'm fixing shish-kabobs."

"I'm over at Mary's house. I wanted to check on Roly," she said. "I'm afraid I'll be here a while."

"Oh," he said, and paused. "How long is a while?" he asked flatly.

"Not quite sure. The baby has an earache or something, and hasn't been able to sleep. Mary's been cooped up for a few days, so I told her and Pete I'd watch him while they went out to supper." Was that a sigh she heard over the phone? "They just went up the road somewhere. I should be home in...an hour and a half?"

"Well, guess I can put these back in the fridge. I just hope no one beats me to the grill." There was more silence. Finally Chase asked, "So how is Roly, anyway?"

"He's been on antibiotics since Sunday, but Mary doesn't think he's much better. He cries every time you lay him down, and he's kind of wheezing. If he's not better by morning she's going to take him back to the doctor."

"I'm sure he's not having any fun." Chase sounded resigned. "Text me when you leave there so I can start the food. I'll see you when you get home."

Laurie tossed her phone back in her purse and glanced at Roly. He was dozing now, his mouth slightly open and his chest rattling. She shifted, her arm almost asleep, and the baby burrowed his head against her shoulder with a whimper.

Twenty minutes later Laurie had to move again. With the recliner still leaning back, she scooted to the edge, threw her legs over the footrest, and turned to snuggle Ricky into a corner in a semi-upright position, propped up with a pillow at this side. She smoothed the damp curls away from his forehead and watched him sleep a moment.

She struggled to her feet over the side of the chair and went to the kitchen for a long drink of water and a look around. Dirty dishes from breakfast and lunch were still in the sink. Making as little noise as possible, Laurie cleared some of the clutter from the kitchen table, loaded the dishes into the nearly-full dishwasher, and turned it on.

She checked on the baby, who was still sleeping. Then she washed a small frying pan and egg-turner she found on the stove. She poured out the last few ounces of coffee left in the carafe since morning, and dumped out the coffee grounds. Finally, she wiped down the table and the counters. Things were starting to look a little better.

Just as she returned to the living room and settled on the couch with the latest edition of Southern Living, the little one started crying. "Oh, nice timing, Roly," she said, tossing aside the magazine and gently letting down the recliner's footrest. "Maybe you're trying to tell me something. Note to self: Motherhood can be very trying." She took the baby in her arms again and, for the next forty minutes, paced the living room.

Chapter 11.

Laurie parked outside her apartment building and peeked through the window of Chase's ground floor unit. Chase sat at the kitchen table with his back to the window. He strummed a few chords on his guitar, paused to write something in a notebook on the table, and then strummed some more.

Chase had written a song called "Climbin' the Walls" as a spoof of Ernest Tubbs' "I'm Walking the Floor Over You," and sent it to a few friends he still had ties to in Nashville. To his surprise, a singer had picked it up and it was gaining a bit of a following. Since then Chase had spent more time composing, hoping to pick up a little extra change.

Laurie walked around to the door and let herself in.

"Am I too late for shish kabobs?" she asked, tossing her purse on the coffee table. "Something smells good in here."

"I missed my chance at the grill outside, so I cooked them in the broiler. Sorry I ate without you. My breakfast was wearing pretty thin."

"Didn't you have any lunch today? You poor baby." Laurie came up behind him and put her arms around his shoulders.

"Well, *somebody* was upset that I didn't come home timely last night, so I made sure I was here tonight."

"You're so sweet," Laurie said, kissing him on the cheek with a loud smack. She came around the table and sat on the chair across from him. "I had to help Mary. She was pathetic. She needed to get out for at least a little while. And unfortunately her babysitter has her own sick kids to deal with. So I minded the baby, and in the ten minutes he actually slept I tidied the kitchen a bit." She looked around at Chase's kitchen.

"Food's in the fridge," he said, and continued plucking on the guitar.

"What's that you're working on?" Laurie asked from behind the refrigerator door.

"I don't know yet. I've had a fragment of a melody on my mind, and I'm trying to work it into something."

"That's the way I am with story ideas. I have a file full of little bits of things. Every now and then one comes in handy." She paused to listen a moment before putting her plate of food in the microwave. "That's a sad-sounding tune you're playing. Beautiful, but sad."

Laurie watched him while the microwave hummed. Finally he set his guitar down and rolled his shoulders. "Did I ever tell you what came into the Treasure Chest the other day?" she asked. "A signed first edition of *Gone With the Wind*."

"Huh," he acknowledged. He closed the notebook he had been scribbling in. "I'm surprised someone would donate something like that. It wasn't a member of St. Mark's, was it?"

"No idea. It was in a box left outside the door. There were some other old books and things in the box. I have a feeling the donor didn't realize what it was." She brought her plate to the table and started eating.

"Well, it will be interesting to see what you all do with that." He reached across the table, grabbed a chunk of meat from her plate, and popped it in his mouth.

"Hey! You had yours. I'm hungry!" She barricaded her plate with one arm. "Yeah, anyway, first we have to find out what the book is worth. Have you ever been to the Margaret Mitchell House up in Atlanta?"

"No. I've seen billboards for it along the interstate though. Or maybe that was for another place. I think there are a couple of *Gone-With-the-Wind*-type attractions up around Jonesboro and Atlanta."

"She was a journalist, you know. I feel like I need to make a pilgrimage, find out what-all we have in common, if anything. Plus maybe the museum could tell us what the book is worth."

"We could drive up Saturday. I promised you I'd be free this weekend." Chase reached for his phone. "What did you call it, again? Margaret Mitchell House?" He searched for info.

"Did you forget? There's a Redding Writers meeting Saturday at ten o'clock. I don't want to miss this one because we'll be talking about the anthology we want to put together."

"Rats! *This* Saturday?" Chase asked, looking annoyed.

Laurie nodded, making a frowny face by way of apology. "We seem to be going in different directions lately."

"Will you still make me pancakes?" He wheedled, giving her that puppy-dog look Laurie couldn't resist.

"That depends on how good you are between now and then."

"Allow me to demonstrate." He came around the table to grab up her empty plate, and as he did so he leaned in and gave her a playful nip on the ear. "Raargh," he growled. "Fresh meat." He nibbled some more.

"Oh, you are hungry, aren't you?"

Chapter 12.

"Hi, Mary." Laurie's phone sounded the next day, and she noted her friend's name on the display before answering. She had been deeply engaged in her work at the *Journal*, and she hadn't noticed it was already mid-morning.

"Aren't you going to ask where I'm calling from?"

"Um, somewhere in the suburbs of greater downtown Chinkapin?"

"Nope. Well, yes. I'm at the hospital."

Laurie bolted up in her chair. "The hospital! What happened? How's Roly?"

"Well, you know that rattling, wheezing sound we were hearing yesterday? Pneumonia."

"Oh, my gosh! So what's happening, then?"

"My poor little one," Mary sighed. "They put this plastic tent-thing over him so they could give him more oxygen."

"Wait. Start at the beginning," Laurie said. "Did you see his pediatrician this morning?"

"Yep, I was there waiting on the doorstep before they opened. Needless to say we didn't get much sleep last night." Mary's tale was interrupted by a big yawn. "Anyway, I told the doctor Ricky just wasn't getting better, even though I was giving him the antibiotics. Of course the doctor listened to his chest and heard all the rattling. They put this little clippy-thing on his finger to measure his oxygen, which was only at around ninety percent what it was supposed to be. That was what clinched it. The doctor sent us to the hospital for X-rays, and the hospital admitted him."

"Poor little thing! I'm so sorry."

"Yeah. Who knew, pneumonia is going around at the school where Melissa's kids go. I had no idea. It seems like the wrong weather for pneumonia." Mary yawned again. "I wish I could have nursed him longer. He might have been safe from all this."

"Just a question," Laurie began, "but – have you and Pete got your pneumonia shots, or flu shots or anything? I mean, do *I* need one?"

"Huh. I don't think we need them, at least pneumonia shots. Guess I should ask someone." There was a pause, and Laurie could hear voices and a soft rustling sound. "Listen, I have to go. There's a tech in the room and I think he's going to do something. I'll text you in a bit."

Laurie stared at her phone a moment after Mary ended the call. *Poor Roly,* she thought. She said a quick prayer for his speedy recovery, and texted Chase to let him know what was up.

She stopped for a quick lunch at home, and then drove over to the county hospital. She got directions at the front desk for the pediatrics ward, rode up in the elevator, and found Mary waiting for her in the hallway.

"Wouldn't you know he just fell asleep," Mary said. "I wish they'd give me a little of whatever they gave him. I could use a nap too."

Laurie walked into the room and looked at Ricky through the plastic tent. "He looks sweaty."

"Yeah, and it'll take a while for the drugs to kick in. The doctor said he'll be here until his lungs clear up some, probably a couple of days at least." The two women sat on a small couch under a window in the baby's room.

"I guess this thing folds out into a bed?" Laurie said looking at the couch.

"Yepper. Don't mess it up. This is where I'll be sleeping tonight. Either me or Pete."

"I don't know why I didn't think of this, but do you need some lunch or anything? I could run out and get you something."

"I checked out the cafeteria. It's not too bad, actually. Pete was here for a couple of hours, and left just a while ago to go back to work, so I did have a bit of a break before you came." Mary went to check on her son. She caressed his arm, and then sat down again.

"You know what's been the worst so far? Watching them suction out Ricky's nose. They stuck a tube up his nose to suck out all the phlegm and gunk."

"Ew," Laurie said with a grimace.

"Yeah, it's as awful as it sounds. He was crying. Pete was still here when they did it, and he made me leave the room, so I went out and paced the halls for a few minutes." She shook her head and continued. "You want to see something else that will break your heart, just walk up and down these halls and check out the kids here. Some of them have family with them, but some are all alone. Right next door is a little girl. I don't know what she's in for, but she looks malnourished to me. A while ago, a motley crew of people came to visit. They made a commotion for about twenty minutes. Then they were gone. Other than that the child has been all alone, except for the hospital staff."

"Sad," Laurie said. A woman in scrubs came in pushing a cart with a monitor and other gadgets on it. Mary got up to watch what was happening, and Laurie stepped into the hall.

She walked along, glancing in through open doors. In one room a woman leaned over a child in a bed. In another, a pair of older adults chatted with a young boy.

Laurie turned around and ambled back past Ricky's room. The door of the next room was open, so she took a step in. She looked right into the bright, round eyes of a little girl. The child was wide awake and sitting up in the bed. Laurie smiled. "How are you today?" she asked, her hands behind her back. The child looked at her curiously, but didn't make a sound.

Laurie tried to judge the child's age. Twelve months, maybe? She looked older than Ricky. Taller, but also leaner. She seemed frail, and as Mary had said, malnourished. There was a ragged sound when she breathed.

A stuffed bear sat at the foot of the child's bed. Laurie picked it up and bounced it up and down, and sang a few lines from a teddy bear song she remembered from elementary school. The little girl followed the movement of the bear, and finally reached for it. "Here you go," Laurie said, handing it over. The child coughed raggedly.

"So this is where you've got to," Mary said, looking in at the door.

"I was just visiting," Laurie answered. "See you later!" She waved at the little girl and followed Mary back next door.

"They just checked Ricky's temperature, which is about normal, finally." Mary yawned again.

"Maybe while he's sleeping you should try to get a nap," Laurie suggested. "Is there anything I can do, or bring you?"

"Not right now. I'll let you know if I think of something. A nap does sound good, if I can get this blind down." Mary hauled away at a small chain to the right of the blind, and the room grew dim. With a parting glance at Ricky, Laurie made her way home.

Chapter 13.

On Saturday Laurie drove up to Redding wishing she had someone riding with her. Chase had given her a pass on the pancakes, and instead had cooked sausage and cheese-grits and added some fresh fruit. They lingered over coffee and then he told her he had some music stuff he wanted to work on, so she was on her own. It wasn't such a long drive from Chinkapin to Redding, but long enough. She had plenty of time to think.

She thought it was a good thing that they each had their own hobbies. Chase was creative, and skillful, and had invested a lot in his music education. She respected what he did, and was glad that he still kept his hand in songwriting, even though he had decided not to pursue a career in performance. He still had connections in the music world, and his songs were gaining attention among some up-and-coming singers.

Still, Laurie wondered whether things would be better if she and Chase had more shared interests.

They seemed to be going in different directions lately. She wished she had a crystal ball to see what the future held for her. Then again, maybe it was better not to know what was coming.

A few years ago she thought she had everything planned out. But even before the divorce, her life had gone seriously off script. It was only in hindsight that she realized the script wasn't right for her at all.

Laurie was through living according to someone else's plan. She was learning to let go of narratives that no longer fit, and was starting to understand what was important to her: faith, love, work, home, family. Mentally she slid the pieces of her life around like tiles in a plastic puzzle that needed to be arranged just right to form the desired picture. They refused to stay where she put them, and the whole picture slid in and out of focus in her mind.

The idea of home kept floating to the top. Laurie thought about cruising past the house she and Chase had seen in the Riverview neighborhood the previous weekend. She was already running late, though, since she had stopped at the Treasure Chest to pick up the old book. She planned to take it to Bookworm after her meeting. She wanted to talk to the proprietor and find out if the book was as valuable as her friends at the thrift shop hoped it was.

Finders Keepers

She found a place to park and swiped her card in the meter to buy a couple of hours. Then she pulled open the door to the Spark Center and headed down the stairs.

The basement of the Spark Center was both an art gallery and a meeting area. It was cool, and smelled a little of paint. She thought of Jeff, her painter friend at the Chinkapin Arts Center, who had once told her that the smell of paint made him relax.

Laurie followed the sound of laughter to where the Redding Writers were gathered at a long meeting table. Her eyes swept the group as she waved to everyone. She knew most of the people from past gatherings, although she couldn't put names to all the faces. One new face surprised her, and this time she remembered his name right away: Luke, from the bookstore in Chinkapin. She would recognize that beard and mustache anywhere.

"Hi. Good to see you found the group," she said, and took a vacant seat next to him.

"It would have been easier if I'd known you met in a basement," he said with a wry smile.

"That was your initiation. Congratulations. You passed the test."

Sydnie, the group's leader, cut through the chit-chat with her commanding voice, honed through years of teaching creative writing to high school students. "Okay, we have about ten items this month, so we need to get cracking if we want to critique them all and still have time to discuss our anthology. Who wants to go first?"

Adarius, who Laurie only knew as a student at the local college, raised his hand. Since all the members were supposed to have reviewed submissions before the meeting, discussion started quickly.

Adarius had submitted a poem about death. Luke looked around, listening to everyone, and Laurie realized he didn't have access to the account where members shared their work. She had her tablet open to the page, and turned it so he could see the screen. He leaned in closer to read the poem.

As the discussion continued, Laurie reached in her bag and silenced her phone. She rarely commented on poetry submissions, other than to say she either liked them or didn't understand them. Even though she loved descriptive, evocative words, her communications background did not prepare her well for analyzing poetry or providing helpful criticism.

Luke didn't seem to have that problem, however. He quickly joined the conversation, inserting thoughtful comments that were well received by the author.

The group continued critiquing members' submissions, and though Luke didn't have time to review them beforehand, he frequently provided insightful opinions. There was even a friendly argument regarding a short story submitted by a guy named Stan. Luke maintained that Stan's story about a rock climber's mysterious disappearance closely paralleled the rumors surrounding the death of a local climbing enthusiast. Stan dismissed his comments until Luke whipped out his phone and found an article in a Georgia outdoors magazine about the event.

"Okay, you guys are going to have to take the discussion outside," Sydnie finally said, "because we have to talk about the anthology."

They spent a few minutes discussing their progress to date on formatting, cover design, and other details. Laurie had a question about her submission, a short essay which really needed an accompanying photo for it to make sense. She took notes as Sydnie provided a helpful website and gave her specifics on how to submit photos.

Laurie was still making notes and copying links while Luke worked with Sydnie to get set up in the system as a contributing member of the group. "So, as far as the anthology goes, I've got two months if I want to submit something?" he asked.

"That's right. What kind of things do you write?" Sydnie asked.

"I'm writing a thriller – a novel. But I was thinking of writing a short companion piece that would work for the anthology, and give me a little advanced publicity for when I launch the book."

"Sounds great," Sydnie said. "Are you hoping to find an agent and go the traditional path, or publish the novel yourself?"

"Probably publish it myself. It seems so easy these days."

"Well, get busy and send in your story! Now that you have access, you'll be able to review the other submissions and see what kind of company you're in." Sydnie and Luke shook hands.

"Thanks. Hey, I really enjoyed this. Glad Laurie told me about the group."

"Glad you found the place," Laurie said as they walked up the stairs together.

Out on the street, Laurie struggled to shove her tablet into her large purse.

"Need me to hold something?" Luke asked.

Laurie smiled. "Here," she said, and handed him her tablet. "I'm always dragging around too much stuff."

As she rummaged and rearranged items in her bag, Luke caught a glimpse of the book she had brought along, and asked to see it. "If you have a minute, we can run over to Bookworm and see if they can give you an opinion on it."

"Yeah! I was planning to try and find it today. Which way is Bookworm?"

"It's a block and a half that way on the next street over." He pointed vaguely up the road. "We can just walk, if you have time left on your meter." He glanced up and down the street, not sure which was her car. Traffic was picking up, and a few people could be seen here and there strolling the sidewalks.

"It's probably about to expire, so.... Want to just ride with me? That way you can navigate. I looked up the address, but I'm still not sure where it is. I'm this little Malibu here." The two climbed into the car and Laurie pulled away from the curb and eased into the traffic.

* * *

"There." Luke pointed. "Park wherever you can find a spot."

Laurie never would have noticed the shop if he hadn't pointed it out. She deftly pulled in – her parallel parking skills had improved greatly since moving to Georgia – and Luke fed a few coins into the meter.

A set of small wind chimes tinkled against the door as Laurie pushed it open and peered inside. An asymmetrical arrangement of shelves extended far back into the shop. She inhaled the smell of old books, along with a faint odor of cat. From the arm of an easy chair in the window, a black and white cat with rounded ears blinked lazily up at her. Laurie perched on the seat and stroked the cat's fur, speaking to it gently.

Luke chatted with a pale, wiry man who was behind the counter sorting and examining books. After a moment, Luke beckoned to her.

"This is K.C.," Luke said, "who is *not* the guy I was telling you about, but he'll take a stab at answering your questions."

Laurie reached across the counter to shake his hand.

"Hey," K.C. said. "Yeah, the person you really need to talk to is Arnie. He owns the shop. But he's out of town for a while – helping his parents move, or something like that, so he'll be gone for a week at least."

"Bummer," Laurie said, shoulders sagging. "Well, let me show you what I have, and maybe you can tell me if you think it's anything to get excited about."

K.C. examined the book, and checked some websites while Laurie and Chase waited, but in the end he didn't tell Laurie much more than she'd been able to find out through her own research. "Your best bet is to get an expert evaluation," he finally said. "Either wait for Arnie, or you could maybe find someone in Atlanta who can authenticate the signature. And if it is authentic, it would be worthwhile to find out something about the person that Mitchell signed the book for. Anything that adds to the provenance would add to its value. That's just not my area of expertise, though. Sorry."

Luke wandered off to browse while Laurie made conversation with K.C. Then she looked at the section of books written by regional authors, and spent a few more minutes with the cat, whose name, she learned, was Cookie.

"Well, that was somewhat helpful," Laurie said to Luke as they walked out of the store together. "I still haven't found out whether what I have is authentic. I did get this, though." K.C. had found her an inexpensive beginners' guide to reading poetry, which she'd bought. "Can I drive you back to your car?"

"Sure, that would be great."

"Hey, I've been meaning to ask you. You know, I do some freelancing for the *Journal*, and I also occasionally have articles published in the *Register*. What do you think about me interviewing you about the bookstore you're opening in Peach Valley? It could be good publicity for your shop." *Plus some parking-meter money for me,* she thought.

Luke didn't need any persuasion. "That would be awesome!" He smiled. "I do some freelance stuff myself, but I knew I couldn't write about my own shop. Can you come to Peach Valley and pay us a visit while we're stocking shelves?"

"Yeah, that would work, and give me some good visuals. The *Register* always likes photos. When would be the best time?"

"Early next week. We'll be working all week getting shelves stocked, with a soft opening on the weekend."

"Awesome. Monday then? Write down that address for me. I've been to Peach Valley once, but can't say I know my way around."

As they drove to where Luke's car was parked, he wrote down the information on a sheet of paper, and handed it to her. She looked it over. "Groovy. I'll see you Monday!"

"Something else I just thought of," he said. "I might be able to get someone from the university to give you an opinion on that book of yours. I'll see if they're willing to take a look at it."

"Sure. Just let me know."

When Luke left, Laurie fished her phone out of her purse, and switched the ringer back on. She was surprised to see two texts from Chase.

Almost thru w/ your meeting?

And then a short while later –

See you at home

She checked her watch. It was after one o'clock and she was starving. She texted Chase.

Headed home – lunch plans?

She stared at her phone a moment, but when she didn't get an answer, she put her Malibu in gear and drove to Chinkapin.

Chapter 14.

"Hi. I'm glad you're home. Have you eaten already?" Laurie let herself in to Chase's apartment, and found him seated at the table with his guitar, plucking out that mournful song he had been working on.

"No. I was waiting for you."

Laurie wondered why he didn't look up. She stared at him a moment, then said, "Well, what are you in the mood for? Want to go somewhere? Or, we could make waffles and eggs. I want to try out that waffle maker I snagged at the Treasure Chest."

"I had hoped to have lunch at the diner in Redding that we liked." He strummed idly, and finally looked up.

"Redding? How was that supposed to happen, when you were working on your music at home?"

"I worked for an hour and a half, and then I drove to Redding to meet you."

"Wait a minute. You drove to Redding?"

"I was going to take you to that diner, and then we were going to try to talk to a realtor about houses in Riverview."

"Oh," Laurie wailed and wrinkled her brow. Chase continued strumming without looking up. "Why didn't you text me?"

"I *did* text you. Right before I saw you come up from the Spark Center and drive off with that...that *person* with the funky mustache."

"That person with the funky mustache is the guy who's going to open the bookstore in Peach Valley. You know, the guy I met at the Franklin's here in town. I want to write an article about the new store opening up. I told you all that last week."

"Well, I don't remember you telling me," Chase said sulkily. "And why would you be meeting a guy from Peach Valley up in Redding anyway?"

Laurie blew out a long breath. She didn't want to argue; not when she and Chase had so little time to spend together these days. "Like I said, he's been working at the Franklin's bookstore in Chinkapin, and since he's also a writer I told him about the group in Redding. I didn't know he would actually show up for the meeting. And I gave the guy a ride to Bookworm, the bookstore on Poplar, just to save him a few steps. I told you about Bookworm last time we went to Redding together. You might remember if you showed a little more interest in me." She wondered if all men were as self-centered as DB. Painful memories of her ex-husband's neglect and indifference crowded into her mind.

"I *am* interested in you," Chase said, exasperated. "Why do you think I came all the way up to Redding to meet you?" He strummed a couple of beats and then set the guitar aside. "Sorry if I'm acting suspicious. I think I'm still kind of shell-shocked after what I went through with Jenny."

Oh, great, Laurie thought. *Now he's comparing me to a screwed-up dead woman. Why doesn't he trust me?*

But the more she thought of it, the less sure she was that she *had* told Chase about Luke.

"I guess you've never been to Bookworm, have you," she said, changing the subject. She sat next to him, and he wrinkled his nose and sneezed.

"No," he said, and sneezed again.

"They sell new and used and even rare books. I was hoping to ask some questions about what to do with the book from the Treasure Chest. But the owner wasn't there today, and the guy who was behind the counter couldn't help me much."

Chase sneezed again. His nose seemed to be getting more stuffed up by the minute. "Does Bookworm have a cat by any chance?"

"Yes. Why?"

He gave her a look that was both comical and pathetic. "I am allergic to cats. Didn't you know that?"

Laurie laughed, and Chase got up and moved away from her, irritated. "I'm sorry," she said. "Is there something I can do? I mean, should I go change or something? I only petted the cat for a minute." She brushed at her clothes, examining her pants for cat hairs.

"It's okay. I'll just take an antihistamine. It's what I have to do when I work an HVAC job where they have cats." He disappeared into his bathroom.

"You're still going to the blessing of the pets with me, aren't you?" Laurie called after him.

"Yes," Chase said, returning with a bottle of pills. He went to the kitchen for a glass of water, and then started rummaging in his refrigerator. "So where's this fancy waffle maker of yours?"

* * *

Sunday morning as Laurie was getting ready for church she texted Mary.

Finders Keepers

How's Roly?

She was surprised when her phone rang and Mary's name popped up on the screen. Laurie put her on speaker so she could continue dressing.

"How's little Roly doing? And how are you? I know it's no fun hanging out at the hospital." Laurie felt a stab of guilt that she hadn't checked on her friend for a couple of days.

"We're a whole lot better. And actually I'm at home. It felt so good to sleep in my own bed! Pete spent the night at the hospital last night, and told me to just come over after church. I'm hoping the doctor will come around and release Ricky today, but nothing seems to happen in a hospital on the weekend. It was as empty as a mall at midnight there yesterday."

"So Roly's over his pneumonia?" Laurie asked.

"Just about. Whatever they're giving him there has done wonders. All the wheezing is gone, and his ears are mostly cleared up. He's been sleeping so much better the last day or so."

"I'm glad to hear it. I guess I'll see you in a bit then."

"Yep. Oh gosh, is it that late? I'd better get a move on. Bye."

Laurie's screen darkened. She finished dressing, and went down the stairs to check on Chase. He was on his couch, guitar in hand. "Hi. Are you ready?"

"I'm waiting on you," he said, jumping up and setting his guitar in the corner.

They parked in the Treasure Chest lot, and as they walked across to the church Laurie could hear a familiar hymn on the organ. The choir started singing the first verse as she topped the stairs to the loft.

Mary was back. Laurie could tell without looking. There was just a fuller sound to the singing, and a richer harmony. She quickly took her seat next to her while Chase went to fiddle with the sound system.

The service began as usual with the procession up to the altar behind the crucifer and the altar servers. Laurie ascended the stairs, careful not to trip on her robe, and they all finished the opening hymn. She turned pages in the hymnal to find the Gloria, which came soon after. Then Mother Barbara read the collect.

As the lector took a moment to find his place for the reading of scripture, Laurie scanned the people in the nave below and idly pondered the whereabouts of a few regulars who were absent. Alice and Don had missed a few services lately, but today it looked like they had a larger-than-usual crowd with them. Laurie couldn't keep up with all their kids, step-kids, and grandkids.

She snapped to attention and reached for a prayer book as the lector announced the psalm appointed for the day, a section of Psalm 46. The congregation began to read in unison. Laurie paused, silently re-reading the fourth verse:

> *There is a river whose streams make glad the city of God, the holy habitation of the Most High.*

She thought those lines had a once-upon-a-time quality about them, like the opening to a story.

> *There is a river whose streams make glad the city of God.*

She loved the sound of it. It was so evocative. She wanted to know more about the river, and the streams, and the glad city. She gave half an ear to the New Testament reading while she read the psalm once more.

Just before the offertory anthem Mother Barbara made her usual announcements about upcoming services and events, and especially reminded everyone about the blessing of the pets that afternoon. It was no surprise, since she had sent an email out to the whole parish a week earlier, but a buzz went through the nave as people asked their friends if they were planning to come. Fair weather was in the forecast, and many were looking forward to the event.

After the service, Steve went to find some extra copies of their anthem for the following week. Choir members took advantage of the break to hang their robes and chat. Laurie stepped into the narthex and found Alice and Don talking to Mother Barbara. Don's eyes met hers, and the conversation stopped so abruptly Laurie wondered what she had interrupted. But Alice took her by the hands and smiled warmly. "The choir sounded wonderful this morning. I just love your music."

"Thanks. We had a full house up there today," Laurie said. "It's great when the whole choir is here."

"And it's nice we have so many men in the choir these days. It didn't always used to be that way. I just love it."

Don took her firmly by the elbow. "Come on, dear, Charlotte's already in the car, and everyone's waiting to go to lunch. We have to hurry, or the Methodists will beat us to the restaurant."

"Right, well, let's go," Alice said, and with a fare-well smile she let Don steer her out the door.

Chapter 15.

"Come on. Let's go!" Laurie hurried Chase out of his apartment and into the car later that afternoon. "What's taking you so long?"

"I had to run back for an antihistamine. I don't know how many cats people will bring to this thing, but I'm not taking any chances."

Laurie and Chase had gone home for a quick lunch after church. Now they drove back to St. Mark's and parked behind the Treasure Chest. A moment later Glenda's van arrived with a couple of helpers from the Chinkapin animal shelter, and Laurie waved them into a parking spot.

As the shelter volunteers helped dogs out of crates and unloaded the van, Chase and Laurie held leashes and calmed the dogs. "We decided not to bring the cats this time," Glenda said. "Since we don't know anything about the other animals that will be here."

"The fewer cats, the better," Chase said pointing to his nose. "Allergies."

The shelter had brought half a dozen adoptable dogs, and Laurie didn't know which she wanted to meet first. She finally settled for an old retriever-shepherd mix, and placed a hand on his back. "I've read that some dogs don't really like to be petted on the head, or want their ears ruffled up."

"That's right," Glenda said. "Not many people know that, but not all dogs want to be petted as much as everyone thinks. A gentle stroke of your fingertips will do, and sometimes they just want to be near you. But the dogs we've brought are all pretty tolerant."

"I'm hoping to take some really cute pictures this afternoon. I already told Scott I was going to write an article for the paper about the pet blessing. Kids and dogs – if anything will get into a newspaper they will."

"That'll be good publicity for the shelter. And look." Glenda pointed to a large goldfish bowl full of dog biscuits. "I brought these along for a little contest. Whoever guesses the number of dog biscuits wins the bowl and all."

They led the dogs over to a shady spot in the church lawn where a table and chairs were set up. Chase crouched down to pet a chiweenie, and Laurie knelt beside him. "Aw, he's adorable!" she said.

"This is just like the dog we had when I was a kid. I don't even think they called them chiweenie's back then. Our dog was just a mutt."

"You had a chiweenie when chiweenie's weren't cool, huh?"

"They're always cool," he said.

"He's so small, though. He wouldn't even make a good squirrel."

Chase gave her a haughty look and then turned back to the dog. "We're going to ignore her, aren't we, buddy," he said, rubbing the little dog's head, which the animal didn't seem to mind. Then Chase grabbed a rubber bone and the two played tug-o-war as Laurie snapped a few pictures.

Mother Barbara arrived with a box of dog biscuits under one arm and a roll of doggie waste bags in her hand. "I remembered these," she said, waving the bags. "Chase, can you please bring around a trash can from the kitchen?" He went to fetch it while Steve brought out a stack of service leaflets and weighted them down with a stone. Other helpers placed bowls of water in the courtyard. "We don't want any thirsty animals falling out," Barbara said.

People continued to arrive, including most of the Treasure Chest volunteers, and a few of the shop's customers who had heard about the pet blessing and wanted to see what went on.

Joan was the only one to bring a cat so far, a very fluffy orange beast in a cat carrier. "What's his name?" Laurie asked poking a finger through the grate on the door.

"This is 'Sweet Potato.' We call him 'Tater.'"

"He doesn't look too happy to be here," Laurie said.

"Well, he's had a rough year, so he's going to get a blessing whether he likes it or not. I told him it'll all be over soon." Joan glanced toward the parking lot, pushed her glasses a little higher up her nose, and narrowed her eyes. "There's Evelyn with that prissy little Maltese. God forbid that dog's paws should ever touch the ground. I think she carries him everywhere."

A Weimaraner, a Welsh corgi, several spaniels and retrievers, and a retired racing greyhound had also arrived with their owners. Laurie looked around for Chase, and saw him chatting with some of Alice's family, who were out in force as they were at the service that morning. He caught Laurie's glance, and rejoined her.

"What a lot of different breeds there are," she commented. "And look at that thing." She nodded toward a coal black dog just coming across the parking lot with its owner. The dog had pointed ears and scruffy, medium length fur that stuck out in all directions. "Too bad we don't have an ugly dog contest," she said. "That thing would take home the prize."

"It looks like it's been rolling in something. Or just crawled out of the swamp," Chase said.

"Or out of a horror film. Is it a dog or a jackal? Let's go check him out."

"This is Max. He's a Mudi," the dog's owner said. "A Hungarian farm dog. They're great herders, but I take Max to agility trials. We have a lot of fun."

Laurie snapped a picture of Max, and then bent to look at one of the prettier dogs, a little girl's poodle. "Tell me about your doggie. May I pet him?"

"This is Bitsy," the girl holding the leash said. "She's a *toy* poodle. That just means she's a little one."

Laurie stroked Bitsy's wooly head. "She sure is pretty. And I love her collar. It's so sparkly."

"I picked it," the girl said. She ran her finger over the rhinestones.

They watched a horse trailer pull in and drive around to park behind the church, expecting to see a horse walk around the side of the building. Instead, a man appeared leading a tiny donkey.

"It's a toy horse!" the girl with the poodle said, dragging poor Bitsy over for a closer look.

"It's a little donkey," Mother Barbara said. "That's like the one that Mary rode on the way to Bethlehem." A mob of children quickly surrounded the animal.

Larry, a dentist, arrived with two kids lugging a glass tank between them. A guinea pig's pink nose stuck out from one end of a wooden tunnel in a corner of the tank, and a round furry rump protruded from the other end. The kids set the tank on the ground and ran to join the crowd around the donkey.

Suddenly a loud squeal erupted as the guinea pig began running in circles. The Weimaraner and the greyhound leaned eagerly over the sides of the tank and followed the guinea pig's every move. Other dogs pricked up their ears and barked, wanting to get in on the action. Larry and Chase quickly raised the tank up out of the way and balanced it on the brick half-wall that ran along the front of the courtyard.

"There's Anne and her grandkids with a birdcage," Laurie said. She went to admire a yellow cockatiel.

"Don't put your finger through the bars," one of the kids said. "Or you'll be sorry." Laurie noted the band-aide on the child's index finger, and snapped a picture of the bird from a safe distance.

She glanced up as a shadow passed over the ground. A large bird circled slowly overhead. Laurie had told Barbara's story of the hawk and the dove to Chase. "That's not a hawk, is it?" she asked.

"That, my dear, is a buzzard. So unless one of these pets keels over and dies, we have nothing to worry about."

Laurie scanned the sky, and looked around anxiously at some of the smaller dogs in time to see the Maltese jump from Evelyn's arms. "Duchess! Duchess, you come back here!" Evelyn shrieked.

Duchess wasn't listening. She raced over to the cockatiel's cage and darted back and forth, barking madly and pawing at the bars looking for an opening. The bird fluttered and screeched as Anne's grandchildren screamed and batted at the dog.

Chase waded in among the children and grabbed Duchess around the middle. The dog barked and waved its legs as Chase carried it to Evelyn. Evelyn held the wiggling dog in both arms and walked off, lecturing Duchess on ladylike behavior. Meanwhile,

Anne lifted the birdcage out of the way and set it on top of the wall near the guinea pig.

Finally most of the animals had settled down. Mother Barbara checked her watch and got the service underway. She nodded at Steve, who stood next to her, and Steve led the crowd singing 'All Things Bright and Beautiful.'

Then Barbara said the opening prayer. "Help us, we pray, to treat with compassion the living creatures entrusted to our care, that they may not suffer from neglect, nor become the victims of any harm; and grant that in caring for them we may find a deeper understanding of your love for all creation. Amen."

The crowd joined in the "amen," which was punctuated by a loud bray from the donkey.

Readings followed, from a creation story in Genesis and then psalm 104. By then dogs whined and strained at leashes, and even the people were getting restless. At last Barbara said, "We recognize the blessing these creatures are to us. Please come forward one by one with your animals so that each may be blessed."

She started with the guinea pig and the cockatiel which were nearest to her. Then people led or coaxed their pets toward her for a blessing and a dog biscuit.

Steve handed out laminated tags which read, "I was blessed at St. Mark's," and people clipped them onto their pet's leash or cage.

"Have I missed anybody?" Barbara called out. When no one answered she said, "Then go in peace to love and serve the Lord."

"Thanks be to God," everyone responded.

"There are plenty more treats. Please stay and visit with our friends from the animal shelter."

People and pets mingled as dogs sniffed each other or gobbled up treats. Laurie snapped more pictures and congratulated Barbara on a successful service. "I was afraid that big bird was going to swoop down and get the poodle or the chiweenie," Laurie said, "but Chase told me it was a buzzard."

"I saw it too. But we're all still alive, thank God, and no blood was drawn, so I'd call the event a success."

"Would you believe someone is already adopting the chiweenie?" Chase said as he joined them.

"That was quick. Guess I'm not surprised though. He is cute! And probably doesn't eat much."

"Maybe we should get a dog," he said.

"What?" Laurie laughed. "Whose apartment would he live in?"

"Mine, I guess. We spend more time there, plus yours is on the third floor. It would be easier to take him outside if he lived in mine." Chase looked appraisingly at the old retriever.

"You've really thought this through, haven't you?" Laurie didn't know what else to say. Her heart warmed at the thought of "we," as in the two of them in a future together. "Maybe we should find a house first. A place with a yard." *Or maybe we should get married first*, she thought. *Or at least engaged.*

"You're right. First things first." He kissed her in front of the church, the animals, and everyone.

Chapter 16.

On Monday Laurie submitted her article about the pet blessing, and had a chat with Scott, the editor at the *Journal*, to pitch her idea for the article on the new bookstore coming to Peach Valley.

Scott was always up for a story on a local business. The *Journal's* subscribers were chiefly interested in local news, the kind that was too far under the radar for the Redding paper to cover. Plus a feature article on a local business might pay off in future ad sales. He told Laurie she could leave work early if she wanted to get the interview.

Laurie found Luke's number on her cell phone, and waited as it rang. She wondered again what Chase must have thought when he saw the two of them drive away after the meeting in Redding. Didn't Chase trust her? He hadn't said anything else about it, but had seemed a bit subdued and very attentive yesterday. Well, Luke didn't mean anything to her. He was an interesting looking guy, though, and Laurie did want to get to know him better. Just to write the article for the paper, of course.

Her thoughts were interrupted when Luke answered the phone. "Hi, Luke. It's Laurie Lanton. I was wondering if this would be a good time to come interview you for that article."

"Sure. I've been moving boxes around all morning. I need an excuse to take a break." There was a smile in his voice, and Laurie imagined the curls on the ends of his mustache curving up.

"Okay, I've got the address, so I'll see you in – oh, thirty minutes or so."

Laurie shoved the papers on her desk into a ragged pile and waved goodbye to Scott. She loaded the address Luke had given her into her navigator, and in a few minutes she was on the other side of the interstate.

Peach Valley was due west, about as many miles away from Chinkapin as Redding was. Laurie enjoyed driving out that way because the cookie-cutter restaurants and stores along the interstate quickly gave way to old farmhouses, fields, and orchards.

The peach orchards which had been in full bloom when she first moved to Georgia were losing their leaves, and looked a bit sad. Meanwhile, the billboards and signs near the packing shed that had advertised fresh peaches earlier in the summer now announced the coming of fresh pecans.

For Laurie's money, there was nothing prettier than a well-groomed orchard. She never got tired of the sight of the pecan groves in the area, which were completely foreign to her northern upbringing. She admired the majestic trees with their sweeping limbs. The grounds around the trees were groomed in anticipation of harvesting pecans in a month or two.

And the cotton! Where Laurie grew up the countryside was full of corn- and soybean-fields. Here, dark green cotton plants stretched row after row, their white bolls gleaming. Laurie was fascinated by them, and curious to see what the cotton harvest would look like.

The scenery changed as Laurie got closer to Peach Valley. The town looked a bit more down on its luck, and not quite as quaint Chinkapin. She crossed the railroad tracks and meandered into town past a gazebo in the middle of a small patch of green.

"Arrived," her navigator's voice said, and Laurie looked around, finally spotting the shop in the middle of a block of old store fronts. She parked half a block up the street and walked back, checking out the other shops as she passed. A barber. A florist. A little restaurant named "Dee's Diner." She crossed an alley, passed a gym, then finally arrived at the bookstore and peered through the glass doors.

There was no mistaking what it was. Tall book shelves lined the walls, and shorter rows of shelves ran down the middle of the store. The children's books were destined for an area in the front, judging by the cheery décor, but those shelves were still bare. Laurie noticed with approval a roomy sitting area with a cushioned bench, a little settee, and several armchairs and small tables near the window.

As she scanned the interior, she saw Luke and a woman, standing close together between two rows of shelves in the middle of the store. Obviously they hadn't noticed anyone outside, because a moment later they were in a passionate embrace, and disappeared behind a display of books. *This is interesting,* Laurie thought. She pulled open the door. "Hello. Is anybody home?"

The woman popped out from behind the shelf holding a book in one hand. With her other she straightened the colorful bandana which covered her hair, tucking in the tight brown curls which peeked out around her neck. "We're not open yet," she called.

Luke reappeared. "It's okay, Cory. I'm expecting her." He rounded the end of the row, now pushing a dolly loaded with boxes. "Hi, Laurie. You got here quick! This is Cory, my temporary employee." He gave Cory a cheesy smile.

Cory rolled her eyes with an audible "humph" and went back to shelving books.

"I guess you didn't have any trouble finding the place," Luke said.

"Not with my navigator, and the name of the shop on the door," she said. "I appreciate that it's painted in big letters."

"I wish the lighted sign were up. I was hoping you could get a picture of it, but the dude from the sign company said he won't be installing it until tomorrow." Luke stopped the dolly and straightened, massaging his lower back.

"That's okay. I like action shots." She smiled at the memory of Luke and Cory's passionate embrace. "Grab hold of the dolly again." Laurie pulled her cell phone from her purse and aimed it at Luke. His face lit with a surprised smile. "Perfect," she said. "Want to give me the nickel tour?"

Luke did the honors as they walked around the store and poked their heads briefly into the stock room in the back. Laurie felt Cory's eyes on her, but when she looked her way and smiled, the woman had returned to stocking shelves.

Luke pointed out the juvenile books section with special pride. "We want to make this really inviting to try to attract families and kids; to get them started on the right track, loving books and reading. We plan to hold different events like story time, special celebrations, author's birthdays and things. Fun stuff."

"I used to want to write kids' novels," Laurie said.

"Kid-lit is in these boxes right here. Take a look." He pulled a handful of books from one of the boxes he had wheeled in, and placed them on a shelf marked 'Ages 9 – 12.' "Series are all the rage for kids. It's almost odd these days to find stand-alone books, at least once you get past the picture books."

"Interesting," Laurie said, flipping pages of a book she had chosen at random. The cover bore a picture of an alien stuck in a puddle of green slime. She placed the book on a shelf. "I have a list of questions I was going to ask. Do you want to take a break so we can sit and chat? It won't take long."

"Well, I didn't bring my lunch. I was thinking of walking over to Dee's just up the block. Want to go with me, and we'll talk there?" He smiled, and Laurie noticed again how his eyes crinkled.

"Sure, that would be fine."

Luke went to speak to Cory, and Laurie walked over to the window to check the view from the front of the store. Reflected in the plate glass, she saw Luke place his hand on Cory's shoulder and give her a lingering kiss. Then he returned and opened the door for Laurie.

"Tell me a little more about Peach Valley," Laurie said as they strolled up the street. "This is only my second time here, and I don't think I got the full sweep of the town, from the route I came in." They passed the gym where a few dedicated athletes trudged away on treadmills.

"There are three things that keep this town alive: the courthouse, the paper-goods factory up the road, and the old college which is down that way." He waved off to the south, and then pulled open the door to Dee's Diner.

A "please seat yourself" sign stood near the entrance. Luke led the way to a table and Laurie followed, looking around at the faded Coca Cola signs on the walls. A waitress swooped in and took their drink orders.

"Speaking of colleges," he continued, "my friend is actually a lit. professor here at the university, and knows something about rare books. I told her about your *Gone With the Wind*, and she's interested in taking a look. She gets over to Chinkapin periodically, and suggested that she just visit your shop one of these days."

"That would be awesome. The sooner the better." Laurie dug in her large purse and found a Treasure Chest business card. "Here are the days and times we're open. I'm there occasionally in the afternoons and on Saturdays, or she can just mention my name and anyone at the shop could show her the book. We'd love to have her opinion."

"Great," Luke said, glancing at the card and stuffing it in his pocked. "But back to Peach Valley: it is what you see, not very big, and not very modern, at least in the center of town here. Things went downhill a little during the economic downturn several years back, but luckily the main economic drivers are not too sensitive to that sort of thing. The town is in a boom of sorts now. There are some new businesses and restaurants along the state route you may have crossed coming in from Chinkapin. Plus we just got a Publix grocery store. That's been a big deal."

The waitress reappeared with their drinks, and took their order. Then Luke resumed.

"A lot of people seem to like the old downtown area, because you can walk here from both the university and the courthouse. There's a burger joint in the next block, and a second-hand furniture store. They're both popular with students. This restaurant actually serves a lot of courthouse people. I'd like to see a good restaurant downtown, or a coffee shop and bakery, but there is a donut shop over toward campus. The more shops that open around town, the more business there will be for everyone."

"Is this a lifelong dream of yours, opening a bookstore?" Laurie had been scribbling notes as he spoke.

"It is, actually. I thought about it a long time before finally making it happen. I've had to make a few trade-offs, and some lifestyle adjustments, but I think it's going to be worth it."

The two talked and Laurie took notes until her sandwich arrived. Then they chatted through lunch. Laurie found Luke an interesting guy. She felt she had a lot in common with him. Like Laurie, he had loved books since he was a child. They allowed him to escape from a chaotic and sometimes confusing world to a place where things made sense. He loved reading adventure stories, where the hero always managed to come out on top despite the obstacles. Luke didn't go into details, but Laurie sensed he had had a tumultuous childhood.

Finally the waitress cleared away their plates, brought a sack containing the carry-out order Luke had ordered for Cory, and left the check. "Let me get this," Luke said.

Laurie protested, offering to pay for her own lunch, but he insisted. "It's my treat. I'm sure I'll more than earn it back from the extra business your article will bring me once we open the bookstore."

Laurie thanked him, and looked over her list of questions one last time. "Just one more thing I wanted to ask. Why Peach Valley? Is this home for you?"

Luke nodded. "It is my home. I moved away for college, lived a while in Atlanta, travelled up in the northeast. But this community and some of the people kept drawing me back. Peach Valley is not a perfect place. Maybe I can make it a little better." He paused. There was an odd expression on his face. Then he hurried on. "Did I tell you? I've just bought the house my grandparents once owned."

"Interesting! I love older homes."

"Me too. I spent a lot of time with my grandparents when I was growing up. Their house was sold when they died, but it recently came back on the market, and I snatched it up."

Laurie studied Luke a moment while his eyes seemed focused on something far away. Finally he came back to the present and smiled, making the curly ends of his mustache curve up even more than usual. Laurie imagined that if his hair ever turned completely white he would make a terrific Santa Claus. "Well, I hope you can get a decent article out of all this rambling," he said.

"Oh, I have plenty of good information." She wanted to ask about his relationship with his "temporary employee," but decided that it was none of her business, especially since it had nothing to do with the article. She glanced at his left hand noting the lack of a wedding band, and involuntarily stroked her left ring-finger with the tip of her thumb.

Remembering Chase's jealousy over the weekend, she decided it was only fair to mention that she was taken, just to be clear about where they stood. As she stuffed her notebook in her big bag she said, "You know, my boyfriend owns an HVAC company." She was surprised at the thrill of pride she felt when she said "my boyfriend" and "owns." "He did a job in Peach Valley recently, and was telling me about some of the older neighborhoods here. I guess there are some nice historic houses in town?"

"There are, actually," Luke said. "I wouldn't say neighborhoods, it's just one area really, but some of the houses are beautiful. And affordable. My grandparents' house, that is, my house, is fairly modest, but it's in the area I mean. If you want to check it out, just follow Main Street to Church Street, and then drive around. The prettiest homes are between Central Avenue and Orchard Street." He grabbed the to-go bag and rolled down the top. "I better get this over to Cory before it's not fit to eat anymore. Like I told you, we're planning the soft opening of the bookstore this Saturday, and then the official grand opening a couple of weeks after that. You'll have to come check it out. There will be giveaways and food and things."

The two shook hands in front of the restaurant and Laurie thanked him for the interview. Luke nodded, gave her a casual salute and walked back to the bookstore.

Laurie checked the map on her tablet and drove around a couple of short blocks admiring the houses, the park, and a small church that caught her eye. Then she drove to the *Register* office to chat with the editor there about her article.

Once back home she wasted no time writing up the story and submitting it to both newspapers. There was nothing to it, really. It was straightforward news, with a little added enthusiasm. She hoped Luke's bookstore would be a big success.

Chapter 17.

Not long after, during her morning coffee break at work Laurie called Mary to check on her godson. Roly continued to improve, but Mary was still keeping him close to home. "Do you think you can work at the thrift shop this afternoon for a couple of hours?" Mary asked. "I know Carol is working today, and Alice is supposed to be with her, but.... You just can't count on Alice."

Laurie agreed to work, and after a quick lunch at home she drove over to the Treasure Chest. She found Carol at the counter.

"Well, hey, girlfriend. I'm glad to see you," Carol said.

"You're not working all by yourself, are you?" Laurie asked.

"Oh, no." Carol followed Laurie into the office and took a seat as Laurie set down her purse. "Evelyn is in the back, pulling out jackets and sweaters. She's doing a whole rack of them. I guess it'll cool down outside eventually. It has been *so* hot. I don't remember it being this hot in October."

Laurie nodded. "Chase and I wanted to eat out at the picnic table near our apartment building last night. We grilled burgers on the little charcoal grill, but then we took them inside to eat. It was just too sticky out."

"So tell me how Mary's little boy is. I saw her in church Sunday, but didn't get to speak to her."

"That's because by the time we get down from the choir loft just about everyone else is gone. I never get to visit. Ricky was a lot better by Sunday, and he finally came home from the hospital Monday."

"Oh, he's home?" Evelyn walked into the office carrying an armload of sweaters.

"Hi, Evelyn. I didn't know you were working today."

"Well that Alice is so darned unreliable. And Mary too, here lately. She's supposed to be here today. I know I saw her in church Sunday."

Laurie tried not to show her irritation as Evelyn criticized her friends. "The only reason she was at church was because Pete was at the hospital with the baby. And Ricky's home now, but Mary's keeping him there. She doesn't want him to have a relapse, or anything."

"He probably got sick because of that babysitter she leaves him with. Here, help me put dates on these tags." Evelyn dumped the sweaters on the work table and returned to the back room for more.

Laurie grabbed a pen and started writing the date on the price tags. "I didn't think Evelyn would be here. Mary asked me to make sure you had a helper. Where *is* Alice today?"

"One of her daughters is in town, the one who lives in Alabama, so Alice is home visiting. She's been doing pretty well, when she remembers to come in." Carol smiled. "But you know, we don't let her handle the money or run the cash register anymore."

"Well, she really wouldn't have to, as long as we have at least two people here. It's nice to have her just talking to the customers. She's so good with people, always friendly and welcoming."

"I guess that comes from her years in the pageants, and with the airline, and everything."

"Pageants? She was in, like, beauty pageants?"

"Oh, yes. She was Miss Georgia back in the day. *Very* glamorous. You should see some of the pictures with the gowns she wore, and everything. And she got married to some big shot from Atlanta, but that was a mistake, and the marriage didn't last long – just long enough for her to have a baby girl. So they were divorced and Alice went back to work. Her parents kept the baby for a while so she could do some modeling, and then she travelled the world as an airline stewardess. That's how she met Don, overseas somewhere."

"Huh," Laurie said. She had forgotten all about dating price tags, and was absorbed in Carol's story.

"I heard it was a big scandal, because Don was in the service – you know, he was a pilot, and he was married. They didn't just look the other way in those days when someone was caught in adultery. It cost him his military career. But then he started flying for the airlines. They still lived up in Atlanta at the time, and Alice still travelled until she had her second daughter. Then she really devoted herself to her family."

"I never knew all that," Laurie said. "I thought she worked in fashion or retail or something."

"That was just for a while, after the kids were grown." Carol sighed. "She's had an exciting life, that's for sure. But I've noticed the change in her lately. She's having a hard time remembering names, and sometimes can't find the words for things. Like we all do, I guess, but I wonder if there's something else going on. Don hasn't said anything."

Finders Keepers

Laurie knew that Alice was forgetful. Still, there had been no change to her personality. Laurie wished she could be as friendly and outgoing. Maybe there was something to this "southern hospitality" after all.

Evelyn returned with some jackets, and looked past the others out the office window. "Oh Lord, here comes that little family." She clicked her tongue. "I don't know what the story is with them, but every time I see that woman I want to give her a bottle of shampoo. And look, the little girl is running through the parking lot without any shoes on."

The bells on the door jangled, and while Laurie finished dating price tags, Evelyn and Carol went out to stand at the counter. Evelyn busied herself neatening up the stack of plastic bags, keeping one eye on the newcomers.

A large plastic bin which the volunteers kept stocked with less-than-perfect toys sat on the floor near the check-out counter. A sign above it read "Free for good boys and girls." The oldest child went straight to the bin. He pawed through the contents, pulling out items to examine and then setting them on the floor. The young woman who Laurie guessed was the children's mother kneeled at the bin beside him.

The barefoot girl stuck three fingers in her mouth and padded down the hallway, glancing backwards to see if anyone was watching. "No, Jessie, stay here," her mother called.

"Look, Jessie." The boy waved a stuffed bear in her direction. He set it on the floor and continued digging, finally pulling out a disjointed robot-toy. With a flick of his wrists he reconfigured the robot into a truck. The woman leafed through a coloring book with some of the pages missing.

Evelyn grabbed an armload of sweaters from the office. Wrinkling her nose, she scooted widely around the little group at the toy bin, and glanced back at Laurie and Carol rolling her eyes. Then she hung and rearranged the sweaters on the rack in the corner.

The man who had accompanied the group pushed through the door with a stroller and placed two coffee mugs on the counter. "These were on the ten-cent table," he said. Then he hollered to the boy. "Jason, go find your little sister!"

Jason ran back along the corridor, and a wail rose up from the direction of the children's clothing room. Laurie peeked around the corner to see Jason leading Jessie away from a plastic riding toy. She struggled from her brother's grasp and pushed the toy up the hallway. Jason looked helplessly up the hall.

"You can't have it, Jessie," her mother said. "Pick something from here. We gotta go!"

Jessie ignored the command. Finally her mother went to pick her up, and carried her back to the checkout counter. "I found you a coloring book, and Jason found you a bear. Now quit your whining." Jessie seemed to forget about the riding toy, and stopped wailing.

Evelyn turned from the sweater rack and raised her eyebrows at Laurie. Silently she mouthed "Two toys?" and raised her palms in a shrug. One toy per child was the rule, though most of the volunteers didn't enforce it.

Carol rang up the mugs on the cash register, and the man handed over a few coins. As Carol wrapped the mugs, Laurie walked over to the stroller to say hi to the littlest child. "How's the little one today?" she asked.

"She's fine. Just has a runny nose," her father answered.

Jason came and put a tiny stuffed rabbit on the plastic tray on the front of the stroller. "Here, Suzy."

The little family left with their items. "Enjoy your afternoon," Laurie said, and watched through the door as they piled into a mangy sedan and drove off.

Evelyn scurried to the staff kitchen and came back with a spray can of air freshener. She spritzed the area around the toy bin, coughed, and waved her hand in the air. Laurie turned away and gazed out the glass door. "Here comes Mother Barbara," she said. The priest exited the side door to the church offices and crossed the parking lot.

The bells on the shop door jangled as Barbara entered. "How goes it at the Treasure Chest today?" she asked.

"Fine as can be," Carol said. "We just made a twenty-three-cent sale."

"Every little bit helps," Barbara said.

"Did you see the family that was just over here, with the three little kids?" Carol asked.

"Yes, I did. I gave them some money for groceries."

"Are they some of your 'frequent flyers?'" Evelyn asked. There were some people who visited Mother Barbara regularly, although she could only offer financial assistance to them once a month. She kept careful track of how her discretionary funds were used.

"Yes, but they really need the help. The good thing is, someone donated them a car, and the man has a new job lined up. But it'll be a struggle until he gets his first paycheck."

"I recognized that little girl in the stroller," Laurie said. "She was in the hospital last week, in the room next to Ricky."

"Really!" Carol said.

"Indeed," Barbara said nodding. "I sat with them one evening when I went to visit Ricky and Pete at the hospital. That child had pneumonia as well."

"I'm sure we'll all be paying their medical bills," Evelyn said.

Barbara narrowed her eyes and gave her a long look. "That man had a good job. He lost it when the last baby was born and his wife had to stay in the hospital for a while. He couldn't work, and visit her, and take care of the other two. Their situation has just spiraled downward since then. At least we can occasionally give them money for food, thanks to the Treasure Chest."

"I wish we could do more - set up a fund for medical emergencies, or something," Carol said.

"Just keep on selling, ladies. Keep on selling."

Chapter 18.

Laurie left closing up the shop to Carol and Evelyn, and drove to the grocery store. She knew there was no coffee left in Chase's apartment. At the store, she always enjoyed the aromas in the coffee aisle, but this time the smell of roasting chickens one aisle over made her mouth water and her stomach growl. She texted Chase to ask if he had plans for dinner, and he agreed that roast chicken was a great idea.

While she waited for the deli crew to remove the chickens from the roaster and bag them for sale, she took a minute to call her little brother. Mike had texted wanting to talk about his trip south.

"Dad doesn't mind if I borrow his truck, and said he'd help me load everything. You sure you want *everything*?" Mike asked.

"Yes. I'm tired of paying rent on that storage unit. Just bring it all down. I'm not really sure what's in all the boxes anymore, but I need my winter stuff, and I'd like my little desk. Whatever else is there, I'll figure out what to do with it once it's down here."

"You do know there was quite a bit of furniture, right? I remember we moved a bed, a dresser, that hope chest...."

"Oh, yeah! I forgot about that," Laurie said.

"How could you forget? We dropped the chest in the front lawn," he said. "My foot was bruised for weeks!"

"Hey, it was a painful time for me too. I've tried to block most of it out."

"I remember," Mike said soothingly. Although he was younger than Laurie, he sometimes acted more like an older brother, responsible and protective. "So how are you really doing these days? Still seeing what's-his-name?"

"Chase," Laurie said. "His name is Chase. And I can see whoever I want." She was suddenly guarded. After all, she and Chase weren't engaged or anything. "I'm doing a lot of writing these days. I've had several articles published in the local paper lately. Plus I'm having fun with the writers group. Two of my short stories will be in the anthology that's coming out next year."

"Uh-huh. That's great. So listen – about timing. I'll probably take two days to drive down, just because I'll have to load up Saturday morning, and then it'll be slow going towing the trailer. So I'll get to your place Sunday around noon. Can your buddy Chase or someone help unload the furniture and everything? Didn't you tell me there's no elevator at your apartment?"

"Yes. He'll help. I'll talk to him."

They hung up and Laurie strolled the aisles of the grocery store another minute. Finally she selected a roasted chicken, and waited in the check-out line.

She drove to the apartment and was surprised to see Chase standing at the door of the building in his bare feet. He didn't notice her pull into the lot and park. He was busy talking to a blonde, who stood a few feet away from him tossing a set of car keys from one hand to the other.

Laurie turned her car radio off and cracked her window open. She was too far away to see the woman very well or hear what they were talking about, but it looked like a serious conversation. The woman was alternately nodding and shaking her head. Chase reached out and placed a hand on her arm. Finally the woman nodded again, turned, and got into her car. As Chase watched the blonde pull out of the parking lot, he noticed Laurie's car, and with a quick wave, he disappeared into the building.

Laurie sat behind the steering wheel wondering. Finally she put her window back up, switched off her car, and went around to the trunk to retrieve her groceries. In a moment Chase was by her side, shoes on his feet, to help her with the bags.

"There you are. I saw you at the door, and then you disappeared," she said.

"I had to get my shoes. I didn't want to walk out here barefoot."

Laurie couldn't resist asking him. "Who was that woman you were talking to?"

"Just someone from church, asking me about some music."

"From St. Mark's?" Laurie had been going to St. Mark's church as long as Chase had, but she didn't recognize the woman.

"Yeah. She was at the pet blessing. She was asking me about writing something for a special service. Hey that sack is ripping." He quickly transferred the bags he was holding to one hand and reached out with the other, but he was too late. The roasted chicken slipped through a hole in the bottom of the grocery bag.

Laurie jumped back as it plopped to the pavement, narrowly missing her shoes. "Oh, man!" she said.

Chase reached down and picked up the chicken, still wrapped in its inner bag. "It's okay. It'll be nice and tender," he said with a smile. "It sure smells good. We still have some corn in the fridge. I thought we could nuke it to go with the chicken."

"Sounds like a plan," Laurie said, still thinking about the blonde. Chase had dropped the subject rather abruptly, but she continued to wonder as he set the bags on the kitchen counter and began rummaging in the refrigerator.

* * *

"You know, I have to work today," Laurie said the following Saturday as Chase talked about the veggies he had in the fridge that could go in their Saturday omelet.

"What?!" He sat up and stared at her, his mouth hanging open. "I thought you worked at the Treasure Chest the *fourth* Saturday."

"I'm working for Mary. Believe me, she'd rather work, but Dragon Lady came to visit – that's what she calls her mother-in-law – and she has to stay home and spend time with her. I would have told you last night, but you had other things on your mind." She smiled and pulled him back down next to her in the bed.

"I did, didn't I." He nuzzled her neck and drew her closer.

"I just said, I have to be at the Treasure Chest at ten o'clock this morning! Now are we going to have breakfast or not?"

"Is that a serious question?" he asked, sliding his hand along her hip.

"I'm hungry! I need coffee!" *And I'm on my monthly, and I have to pee,* Laurie thought.

"Okay, okay. I'll start chopping. You jump in the shower."

Once out of the shower Laurie threw on yesterday's clothes and squeezed past Chase to pour herself a mug of coffee. Diced onion, bell pepper and ham sizzled in the skillet as Chase whipped eggs in a bowl. "Smells delicious," she said. "I'm running up to my place to change. Be back in a tick."

She scampered up to her third floor apartment thinking about ticks. She was glad the summer was over. Soon there would be far fewer mosquitos, gnats, and ticks to worry about. Everyone was hoping for a cold winter to kill off some of the bugs. It looked like it had finally cooled off and turned into gorgeous fall.

Laurie loved fall, and Hallowe'en, and what Chase called the "spidering" time of the year. Big banana spiders could be seen outdoors, their huge webs strung across doorways and along porches, from shrubbery to tree to fence, and often right where you could walk into them before noticing they were there. Laurie appreciated any creature that ate bugs, and loved to see their elaborate webs, but did hate walking through them. She had started being very careful before she crossed a porch or a lawn. She knew the spiders themselves weren't dangerous – unless you threw your back out trying to avoid them.

Dressed and with her brown hair spun into a French twist, Laurie returned to Chase's apartment.

"Just in time," he said. "Strawberry jam or apple butter?" He was placing a plate of toast on the table, next to a bowl of steaming eggs scrambled with lots of veggies and a bit of leftover sausage.

"Apple butter. I've been thinking about fall. Apple anything sounds really good." She had just spread apple butter on a piece of toast when her phone rang.

Laurie swiped the screen and tapped the speaker button. "Hello, Mike," she said. "How's everything going?"

"Wanted to let you know, everything's packed, and I'm hitting the road as soon as I hang up. Dad says to be careful with his truck and drive slow, so I'll see you in about a week."

In the background Laurie could hear her father's voice call, "Hello, Pumpkin."

"Hi, Dad," Laurie answered. "Seriously, Mike. Are you still hoping to be here around noon tomorrow?"

"That's the plan, if I can make it at least as far as Knoxville this evening."

"Okay. We'll feed you lunch, then." Laurie looked up at Chase, who nodded agreement. "Gotta keep you fueled up so you can move that furniture."

"Yeah, and hopefully your friend what's-his-name can help with the unloading."

Chase rolled his eyes, but smiled and nodded. "What's-his-name will be here. No worries."

They finished breakfast and Laurie started to help Chase clear away the plates. "Just go," he said. "This is how you always make yourself late."

"I'll be home shortly after 2:00. Do we have plans for this afternoon?"

"Want to drive over to Peach Valley? You said you wanted to go back and look at some of the neighborhoods there."

"Yes! That sounds like fun. See you!"

Laurie arrived a minute before opening time at the Treasure Chest. As usual Virginia had beat her there. She was counting the money for openers into the cash drawer.

"Hi," Laurie said. "You got all the lights on?"

"I do." Under her breath Virginia counted pennies, slid them into the drawer, and made a note on a pad of paper before looking up. "Fifty, on the nose. You can put some music on, if you like."

Laurie went to the staff kitchen, put a CD into the boom box, and adjusted the volume.

"Anything on sale today?"

"Just the books-on-tape, as usual," Virginia said. "Evelyn said not to put anything else on sale. But we really need to get one of the back rooms cleaned out soon. In a month or so we're going to want to set out all the Christmas stuff."

"Hmmm," Laurie tapped her chin with a marker, looking at the dry-erase board at the front of the store where sales were listed. "I see lots of blank space on this board. What do you think about a flash-sale on kitchen items: everything half price?" Virginia smiled at her, and Laurie wrote a note on the board. "Just remind me to erase this before we leave this afternoon!" The two exchanged a high-five.

Laurie looked around the store to see if anything needed replenishing. "The display in the hallway looks really nice," she said, admiring the pumpkins and fall décor on the shelf. "I thought we had more fall stuff than this, though."

"There are some Thanksgiving items in the cupboards."

"We should probably put those out. But didn't we have some Halloween shirts and costumes in the back room? I'll go look."

The women busied themselves bringing out more items for sale. As they worked, Virginia chattered on about her family, other Treasure Chest volunteers, and thrift shop customers. There were customers they could count on coming in on a regular basis, but a few newcomers always discovered the shop whenever there was a dog show or livestock event at the nearby fairgrounds.

The bells on the door jangled, and Laurie returned to the counter to find Evelyn walking into the office. "Evelyn! I'm surprised to see you here!"

"It's my turn to set up the altar for Sunday," Evelyn said. "I just finished next door and thought I'd stop over here to see how it's going."

Laurie fought the urge to glance at the dry-erase board. She didn't want to draw attention to the sale on kitchen items she had added. Evelyn apparently hadn't noticed it. Laurie took her chance to erase it when Evelyn got a call on her cell phone and lingered in the office to answer.

The shop was relatively quiet until several children burst in, followed by an old man who shuffled to the chair near the counter and sat down heavily. The man's legs were badly swollen.

"I wonder if you have some pants that would fit me," he said.

"I bet we do," Virginia said. "What's your size? Are you looking for any color in particular? Blue jeans? Khakis? Dark pants?" She got the details from him and scurried to the men's clothing room to see what they had.

While Virginia was busy looking, the children ran back and forth to show the man items of interest they found in the toy aisle. Evelyn wandered toward the back of the store, keeping an eye on the kids.

"I bet these little ones keep you hopping," Laurie said, and then regretted her choice of words considering that hopping was probably not something the old man could manage.

"Oh, I have diabetes, you know, which makes it hard to get around, but the kids help me out quite a bit." He stopped to admire a baseball glove a boy brought to show him.

The boy scampered back to see what else he could find, and the man turned again to Laurie. "There's four grandkids under the age of eight. My daughter works the weekends, and my son-in-law works twelve-hour shifts, so I help them out. We all look out for each other. They're good kids, and they love their Paw-paw." The boy came back with a bicycle helmet. "What do you tell me when I go for a cookie?" he asked the boy.

The child smiled and pointed. "Paw-paw: in the corner!" He leaned against the old man's knee. "And when we're bad, Paw-paw says 'You want to take it outside?'"

The man put an arm around the boy and admired the bike helmet.

"I found these," Virginia said, returning with four pair of pants. "You tell me if you like any of them. This one is pretty heavy – might be good for the colder weather that's coming."

He checked the sizes, and examined the pants. Meanwhile, the kids each came to him with toys for his approval. "Just one, Tammy," he said to a little girl who brought three stuffed animals.

"I really like both of these." The man indicated two pair of pants. "Let's see what my total is so far." The kids crowded around him and placed their selections on the counter. As Evelyn observed from across the room, Virginia checked the tags on each item, punching the keys on the calculator. "The toys come to seven dollars, and the pants are three dollars each."

The man's face worked as he did some mental arithmetic. From his expression Laurie guessed the numbers added up to more money than he had with him. "Weren't we running a 'buy one-get one' special on men's pants?" she asked.

Virginia hesitated a moment, glancing back at Evelyn who raised her eyebrows. "Oh, yeah!" Virginia said. "So your total comes to ten dollars plus tax." Evelyn left the room tight-lipped, shaking her head.

The man was visibly relieved. "All right! Here's ten dollars." He leaned over in the chair and pulled a crumpled bill out of his pants pocket, and handed it to the oldest boy, who gave it to Virginia.

"And let's see. The tax would be...." He pulled out a couple of quarters, placed them in the boy's palm, and dug in his pocket some more.

"That's enough," Virginia said. "The last person left their change, so it'll come out exactly right."

The boy smiled, handing over the two quarters. Virginia rang the sale up on the cash register while Laurie bagged the pants. The children grabbed their toys and started chattering noisily. "You-uns go outside and wait for me. You're raising too much racket." The man rose slowly from the chair and took his package. "Thank you. You ladies have a nice day, now."

"We will. Come see us again," Virginia told him.

He made his way slowly to his car. Laurie stood at the open door enjoying the afternoon air as another car pulled into a parking space. "Here comes Don. Looks like he has a donation for us."

Don entered carrying a cardboard box. Laurie usually felt like she should stand up straighter whenever Don was around. Tall and fit, he was always well-groomed and steely-eyed. Laurie could easily imagine him in his military flight suit, striding out to take his place in the cockpit of a jet.

Today he seemed different. He stooped slightly, and looked tired. He set the box on the counter, and took the seat recently vacated by Paw-paw.

"Hi, Don. Good to see you. What have you got for us?" Laurie kept one eye on Don as Virginia unloaded the box.

"Alice and her daughter have been going through a few closets. They found these purses Alice hasn't used in a while, and thought you might be able to sell them." He leaned back in the chair and closed his eyes.

Laurie was sure they could sell them. She knew Alice appreciated quality clothing and accessories, and took good care of them. Evelyn appeared from nowhere and started looking over the items. "Oh, these are nice," she agreed. "These will sell fast." She stepped into the office for some tags before the others could price them too low.

Don opened his eyes again and addressed Laurie. "I sure do appreciate that boyfriend of yours helping me out with my heating system. I was afraid I was going to have to replace the whole shebang, but I mentioned it to Chase and he thought it was just a small problem. He was right on the money." Don laughed. "Didn't charge me any, either! That house gets as cold as a tomb when the weather turns chilly." A cloud seemed to pass over his face, and Laurie shivered at the image his words had created in her mind.

Don seemed to feel the same. He looked at the women, as if trying to think of something more cheerful to say. "How's business today?" he asked finally.

"A little slow for a Saturday," Laurie answered. "It's tempting to close early on a day like this, but sometimes at the last minute someone will come in and spend fifty dollars. You just never know." He nodded, and rose from the chair.

Laurie had the feeling there was something else on his mind – something he wanted to say. "So Alice's daughter is still visiting?" she asked.

"She is. They're catching up. Girl talk, and just poking around the house. I had to get away before they put me to work. They only let me escape because I agreed to bring you that box." He stood with one hand on the counter.

"We appreciate it, Don," Evelyn said, bustling back and forth and hanging the purses where shoppers would see them.

"Take care, then. I hope you get a few more customers." He straightened, and with a nod he left the shop.

"He didn't seem very spunky today, did he," Virginia commented.

"*Spunky*," Laurie repeated. "He's never been exactly the spunky type, but I know what you mean."

"Maybe Alice's daughter has out-stayed her welcome," Evelyn suggested sarcastically.

Laurie shook her head. She dug her phone out of her pocket and snapped a picture of the purses on display.

"What are you doing?" Evelyn asked suspiciously.

"Just taking a picture so I can advertise these purses." She let out a sigh and glanced at Virginia who just smiled back. Laurie opened Facebook and posted the photo along with some text:

Finally got your stuff together but don't know where to put it? Shop the Treasure Chest for a great new purse! We have lots of beauties on sale now.

Two of Alice's purses sold that afternoon. As Virginia totaled up sales and counted the money in the cash drawer, Laurie walked through the Treasure Chest turning off lights. She checked the thermostat, thinking about Don. Chase hadn't mentioned anything about helping him out with a heater problem. Come to think of it, she didn't even know where Don and Alice lived.

She still felt like there had been something else on Don's mind. He had looked older – but then wasn't half the parish getting older? Maybe that was why Alice's daughter was spending time with them.

Laurie paused in the toy aisle to pick up a stuffed giraffe one of Paw-paw's grandchildren had brought to him that morning and then rejected. The kids were lucky just to know their Paw-paw, these days when families were so scattered. As she placed the giraffe on the shelf she wondered how often he stole a cookie and was ordered to stand in the corner. She hoped their family would be together for a very long time.

Chapter 19.

Laurie helped Virginia lock up at the Treasure Chest and then she drove to her apartment. From the hallway outside Chase's door she could hear his guitar, and quietly let herself in.

He sat on the couch with his instrument across his lap, his notebook on the table beside him. Laurie guessed he'd been composing again. He set everything aside and rose to envelope her in a hug. "Great day at the Treasure Chest? Let me guess - you made six hundred dollars today."

"Not even close, but we did break a hundred, which is good enough for a Saturday. Is there any chicken left? I think I've had too much coffee this morning. Either that, or there actually is a hole in my stomach."

"Who wants old leftover chicken when we can go to the packing shed and get a fresh pecan roll? I'll drive so you can enjoy the scenery."

"Ooh, you talked me into it, you sweet-talker, you. Let's go."

It was a nice afternoon for a drive – finally cooler, with no humidity and an intensely blue sky. Laurie wished the weather would stay that way for the rest of the year.

The packing shed Chase headed for was the largest of several peach packing houses between Chinkapin and Peach Valley. Known simply as "the shed" to the locals, it had started as a humble warehouse operation that geared up a couple of times a year to accommodate the peach and pecan harvests. Over time it had grown into a large produce market, bakery, and tourist destination.

"My elementary school took us on a field trip to a packing shed once," Chase said. "We got to watch the crew sort the peaches by size and cull the bad ones, and then we all got a peach ice cream cone. And every year my mom would buy a box of peaches to put up in the freezer. There's nothing like sweet, frozen peaches in the middle of the summer. We used to eat them instead of popsicles."

"So you were a foodie even as a kid," Laurie said.

"I guess I was. Or just lucky."

They found a spot at the far end of the crowded parking lot, and walked past a small playground featuring old tractors for kids to climb on. In the distance Laurie saw rows of vines trained on tall arbors.

"What's growing back there? Is that just grapes?" Laurie asked.

"Muscadines and scuppernongs, probably."

"You're making that up, right? Scuppernongs? Is that really a word?" Laurie looked at him suspiciously.

"I am not making it up."

Laurie shook her head and rolled her eyes with a smile. Suddenly he grabbed her hand and pulled her past the playground down to the arbors for a closer look.

"OMG!" she said. "Look how big and round they are. I've never seen these before." Under her breath she read the label at the end of the arbor. "I guess these are, like, demonstration gardens."

"Or they grow them to sell in the market, and make jelly and wine out of." Chase gave her a look that clearly said, "as everyone knows."

"Well, I've never heard of them before. What do they taste like?"

Chase plucked one off the vine. "The skins are tough and sour, so you just suck out the insides and spit out the skin."

Laurie looked uncertain, but did what he described. "Oh, sweet!" she said. She tried chewing on another one. "I see what you mean about the skins.

Yuck." She spit the tough skin out on the ground. "These vines are really beautiful."

They walked farther down along the rows. Yard after yard of various plants were strung along wires supported by stout wooden posts. "These look like raspberries," Laurie said.

"Blackberries, probably," Chase told her. "Hey, look over here."

"Kiwis!" she exclaimed. "I didn't know kiwis grew here! I thought they all came from New Zealand, or somewhere. Look, big bunches of them!" Laurie was fascinated, and took several pictures with her cell phone. "These are awesome. How cool would it be to grow these in your back yard? You know, there's a story here. I've got to tell Scott about this."

"That's probably a good idea." Chase watched smiling as she snapped a few more pictures.

"But now I really am starving," she said. "Let's go up to the market."

After a deliciously balanced lunch of pecan pie for appetizer, barbecue sandwich for the main entrée and peach ice cream for dessert, Laurie and Chase got back on the road to Peach Valley with a trunk full of fresh fruit and a few bakery items for tomorrow's lunch with Laurie's brother.

Finders Keepers

"So where was the job you worked out here?" Laurie asked as they drove into town.

"The new grocery store. It's near the fast food places on the east side. Not a very interesting part of town, unless you live here, of course. Then a new grocery store *is* probably interesting."

They turned south and drove past the university. Laurie studied what she could see from the main road.

"Doesn't look like a lot of people around here, for a college town."

"Well, it is Saturday," Chase said. "Let's go past the courthouse, and then we'll drive through some of the neighborhoods."

They turned and followed the road through the small downtown. "Look." Laurie pointed. "There's the new bookstore." Chase drove slowly, looking out the window. Laurie craned around as they passed. "Looks like a few people in there. And there's the restaurant where Luke and I had lunch."

Chase glanced quickly at Laurie, and she regretted her choice of words. "You know, where we did the interview," she said. She kept her eyes straight ahead, hoping he didn't see her blush. Chase drove on without comment.

Laurie reminded herself that there was nothing wrong about a working lunch with someone she was interviewing for a newspaper article. She felt suddenly irritated, remembering how upset Chase had been when she'd gone to Bookworm with Luke.

She wondered about the woman Chase had been talking to outside their apartment building the other day. Someone from church, he had said, but Laurie certainly hadn't ever met her. She wanted to ask Chase about her, but decided against it. She didn't want to seem jealous. She slid down in her seat, frowning.

Chase brought her out of her reverie. "Look, there's the Episcopal church in Peach Valley, St. Bartholomew's. Looks narrow, doesn't it?"

"But...there was an Episcopal church across from the college. We passed it back there. St. Michael and All Angels, or something."

"Right, well that's the thing about Peach Valley. The town has an interesting history. The university here is what they call an HBCU, which stands for historically black colleges and universities. And St. Michael's was the black church."

"Two Episcopal churches in one small town? That's unusual, isn't it?"

"Not really."

"But why don't they just combine?"

"That's what the diocese wants, but – you're opening a whole can of worms. This is the South, remember."

"Hmph," Laurie thought. She remembered, but she didn't really understand. Her upbringing often didn't prepare her for reality, and her ignorance made her feel uneasy.

"Okay," Chase said, slowing down. "Look at this little park. This is the neighborhood I was thinking of. Look at that house. What a great porch."

"Ooh," Laurie breathed. "I love the woodwork! And the big old trees. They've been here forever." They drove on, and passed several more houses that were easily over one hundred twenty years old. "I'm not seeing any 'for sale' signs, though."

They circled the block. Finally Laurie said, "Let's park and take a walk. I need a little exercise after that nutritious lunch we had."

Chase pulled into a side street and parked, and the two walked back to the square. As they strolled along they admired brick walkways, old gardens, and all the interesting architecture.

"Look at how many chimneys this house has," Laurie said.

"A fireplace in each room, probably. That's a lot of ashes to haul. Bet that place is a nightmare to heat and cool. If they even have air-conditioning."

"Chase, I love you, but I'm not living in a house in Georgia that doesn't have air conditioning." Laurie thought again about the fact that they weren't engaged yet.

"Hey, you're the one who wants one of these old houses."

"I love the looks of them. I *think* I want one." Laurie actually wasn't sure what she wanted. Some days she desperately wanted marriage and a family. Other days she was focused on her career, and enjoyed being out in the world meeting interesting people and uncovering stories to write about.

Chase grabbed her hand. "There's a nice one," he said, pointing.

"I like the row of dogwoods along the walkway," Laurie said. "I wonder what it would be like to live in Peach Valley."

"Well, at least they have a new grocery store." Chase smiled.

"And a bookstore!" Laurie added.

"But seriously, you'd probably have to drive up to Redding or over to Chinkapin or somewhere when you wanted to really shop, or go to a movie, or anything else. I don't know if there's even a good coffee shop here."

"Luke said there was a donut shop, but not really a coffee shop, unless there's something on campus. I might feel old hanging out with a bunch of college students, though. I like the mix of people we see in Chinkapin."

"I'm sure there's a mix here too," Chase said.

They had circled the park and arrived back at their car. "Now what do you want to do?" Laurie asked.

"I bet you've never been to Springwood Gardens."

"At least I've heard of Springwood. Isn't that the camellia place? Is it near here?"

"Just about a fifteen minute drive."

"Is there anything to see there? It's not really camellia time, is it?"

"No, but it's a pretty place, even in the off-season," Chase said. "Let's go, just so you can get an idea."

They climbed back in the car and headed south, and were soon surrounded by countryside again. "Some of these pecan orchards are huge," Laurie said.

"Yep. People tend to forget that most of south Georgia is all about agriculture. You just don't see it unless you get away from the interstate and start driving around."

Laurie looked out the window at a train rolling past, and noticed a sign with an arrow pointing toward the garden. They turned, and there was a sprawling brick Georgian building, looking distinctly incongruous in the rural landscape. Chase pulled into the drive and parked near a large fountain.

"What a beautiful building. It looks like it's closed, though," Laurie said looking toward the entrance.

"We'll come back sometime so you can see inside," Chase said. "Today we'll just sneak into the garden."

"Is it all right, do you think?" Laurie asked. They seemed to be the only ones around.

"I've done it once before," Chase said leading her down the path.

Laurie didn't have the nerve to ask if he had done it with another girlfriend, or maybe his late wife. She wondered if he still missed her. After all, she'd only been dead for...how long? Laurie wasn't sure. Or maybe Chase just felt relief, considering the problems the woman had caused. Or regret, for what might have been.

Laurie stopped thinking about the past. She felt like she'd just walked into a florist's shop. The air was still and fresh under the towering pines. Pine straw carpeted the brick walkways, which sectioned off gardens filled with camellias of all types.

Most of the shrubs were marked with name tags, and Laurie liked the more evocative ones, like King's Ransom, October Affair, and Raspberry Ice. Many were covered with fat buds, and some were already in bloom. "I thought all camellias bloomed in the winter," she said, admiring a fluffy pink blossom. "This place will probably be gorgeous in another few months."

"It will be gorgeous. Different varieties bloom at different times, some as early as October or November. But others won't bloom until later. There's a big festival here in February."

"We'll have to come back. I had no idea this was so close to where we live, and so big. Georgia is just full of hidden treasures, isn't it."

"I am. I mean, it is," Chase said playfully. He took her hand. "Come this way. I want to show you something."

He led her to a wooden shelter at the entrance of a Japanese garden with a koi pond. She sat on a bench in the cozy shelter while Chase crossed the pond on small millstones placed as stepping stones. She admired his athletic body as he stepped lightly across and then turned, looking down into the water. "Some of these koi look pretty tasty. Bigger than pan-size," he said.

Laurie laughed. "Good thing we already had lunch. Aren't koi supposed to be very bony, actually?"

"I have no idea. I just think they're pretty to watch."

Laurie left her perch and joined him at the edge of the pond. Dark green lily pads floated on the water, with here and there a blossom. "Golly, they are huge," she agreed.

As they left, Chase struck a small steel gong near the entrance to the little garden. "You just called the gods," Laurie said. "You should bow."

"Huh?"

Laurie bowed twice, slowly from the waist, while he looked on. Then she closed her eyes. She said a quiet prayer for future happiness, wondering where their house-hunting would lead. Then she clapped twice and opened her eyes. Chase stared at her, hands on hips.

"I had a friend in college who practiced the Shinto religion." She shrugged and smiled. "This looks like a holy place."

Chase took her hand again, and pulled her toward him. "Are we allowed to kiss in a holy place?" He kissed her gently on the lips.

"I never heard that you weren't," she said, placing her arms around his neck and pulling his face closer to hers.

He looked into her eyes, and kissed her again. "Come on," he said. "There's something else here that you should see."

They held hands, walking slowly along the path which parted to circle around what looked like a small brick house. In the center of a square parterre garden was a multi-tiered metal fountain with swans decorating its base. As the water fell from tier to tier it made a melodic plinking sound. Laurie cocked her head to listen.

They sat on a garden bench and watched the water spill from the edges of the fountain into the basin below. "How peaceful this is. What a beautiful place." Laurie closed her eyes and listened as a light breeze whispered in the pines. It was getting cooler. She snuggled close to Chase, and leaned her head on his shoulder.

After a while he shook her gently. "Hey. Did you fall asleep?"

"No. It just felt so perfect here I didn't want to move. It's getting chilly, though. Come on." She got up from the bench and started sleepily in the wrong direction.

"Hey. The car's this way." They walked in silence for a moment. Then he said, "And speaking of chilly, I'm hungry. What do you think about chili for supper tonight? While I'm at it, I'll throw something together that we can have with your brother tomorrow."

"I love a man who cooks," Laurie said, feeling very blessed indeed.

Chapter 20.

Sunday morning after the church service Laurie's cell phone rang as if on cue. She fished it out of her purse and saw Mike's name on the screen.

"Hi, Bro. Where are you?"

"According to the nav I'm about thirty minutes out. I had to stop for gas, and my stomach is telling me it's lunch time. You still planning to feed me?"

"I'll feed you. You still like bologna, right?" she teased. "Seriously, just come on over to my apartment."

"Okay. See you soon."

He hung up, and Laurie turned to Chase. "That was Mike. He'll be at my place in about thirty minutes."

"Better get going, then."

At her apartment, Laurie heated up the enchiladas and rice Chase had prepared the night before, and got out some tortilla chips. "I'm not sure all this goes together," she said, looking at the plate of bakery items they had bought at the shed the day before.

"It'll be fine," Chase said, adding the salsa he had fetched from his refrigerator.

Through the window Laurie spotted her dad's old blue pick-up pulling into the lot, and ran down the stairs to let her brother in.

Once in her apartment Laurie introduced him to Chase, and the two men sized each other up. Mike was taller by at least three inches, and Laurie thought he had put on a few pounds. Not that he looked bad, by any means. But she did think Chase looked more fit, probably due to the physical labor he frequently did. And Chase did look good in the olive green polo shirt he was wearing. She was glad she had been able to convince him not to change into a tee shirt after church.

"So, Chase. Do you play golf?" Mike asked.

"No, not at all. Not much into sports," Chase said.

"Too bad. I was thinking of driving over to Augusta while I'm down here," Mike said. Laurie thought he sounded a bit pompous, especially since he had only recently learned which end of the golf club to hit the ball with. But she figured he was trying to find out whether Chase was good enough for her.

"What'll you have to drink, Mike?" Laurie asked.

"How about a Pepsi? I've been drinking coffee all morning."

"You're in luck, Bro. Although you are now deep in the heart of Coca-Cola country, I picked up some Pepsis at the grocery store just for you."

"What kind of work do you do?" Mike continued trying to figure out his sister's new boyfriend.

"HVAC sales, service, and installation," Chase answered simply.

"He'll be the owner of the company, once he buys out...the other guy," Laurie said. She was proud of what Chase did, but didn't want to get into the messy details about him buying the business from his one-time father-in-law.

"Sounds like a good business to be in," Mike said. "I can't believe how warm it is down here."

"Our busy season is really just winding down," Chase said.

"It'll be a little cooler in Atlanta," Laurie remarked.

They worked their way through their food. "Good enchiladas," Mike remarked looking at Laurie.

"Chase made them," she quickly pointed out. "He's a really good cook."

"Is he, now," Mike said glancing at Chase. He seemed tickled by the idea. Or maybe he was just amused by how hard Laurie was trying. She turned red in the face, and got up to cool off and refresh their drinks. Laurie thought about her ex, and couldn't remember anything he ever cooked particularly well, other than hot dogs. She was still thinking about DB when Mike asked, "So how did the two of you meet?"

"In choir, at St. Mark's," Chase said.

Mike looked at Laurie. "Choir? I didn't know you were that interested in singing."

"Mary got me into it."

"That makes sense," Mike nodded. "I remember her being in all the concerts in high school." Although Mike was a couple of years behind Laurie in school, the two had sometimes hung out together, and had a few friends in common.

"You'll be seeing Mary in a bit. I convinced her to let me store some of my furniture in her garage."

"So you're a singer, are you Chase?" Mike asked.

"I have a degree in music composition."

"Really!" Mike sounded a bit more impressed. "What type of music do you compose?"

"Popular contemporary, country, some jazz. A variety, really. My main instrument is guitar."

"He's had a couple of songs picked up by Trey McGann," Laurie said. "I don't know if you've ever heard of him."

"Sounds like a country singer," Mike said dismissively. "One of my co-workers listens to that stuff all the time. I don't listen to it that much."

"Have you heard 'Climbin' the Walls' or 'Nabob in Nighttown'?" Laurie waited to see if either of those rang a bell.

"Wait a minute," Mike said, his eyebrows rising. "You wrote 'Nabob in Nighttown?'" He looked disbelievingly at Chase, pulled out his phone, and started searching. Then he read from the screen, "'Written by C.W. Harris.' That's you? What does C.W. stand for – Country and Western?"

"Oh, God!" Laurie said rolling her eyes.

"It's Charles Wesley Harris, at your service." Chase nodded formally. Then he threw up his hands and shrugged. "For some reason my serious songs never get any traction. But if I toss off something as a gag," he pointed emphatically, "that's the one that makes it."

"They've been playing the hell out of that song. In fact I heard it a while ago at the convenient store when I stopped for gas." Now Mike had an amused smile on his face. "How come you're not doing music full time?"

"Been there, done that," Chase shook his head and looked away. "It's fun for a while, but it's a really hard way to make a living. Plus it's hard to have any kind of family life in the music business."

Mike glanced from Chase to Laurie and back to Chase. Laurie started clearing plates, careful not to meet Mike's eyes.

"Well, what do you think?" Mike asked. "Ready to go down and unload whatever you want to keep here, and then drive over to Mary's place?"

"Sure," Laurie said. "Let's get started. I want to look in some of the boxes before you drag them up the stairs."

In the end two boxes of books went straight into Laurie's closet. Four other boxes ended up stacked in her bedroom. Laurie knew they were full of winter clothes and a quilt or two.

Mike and Chase seemed to be in competition to see who could carry more items up the stairs. Mike had longer legs, and occasionally took the stairs two at time, but Chase was the stronger of the two. The men worked together to bring up Laurie's desk, and had to move her couch several inches so the desk would fit into a corner of the living room. Laurie carried the drawers up one at a time.

"Grandma's desk! I'm so glad to have it back again!" It was a charming old secretary with three lower drawers and chubby, curved feet. A slanting top opened to form a work surface, revealing of row of cubbyholes for papers and supplies. Mike watched as Laurie carefully slid each of the lower drawers into place. Then she lowered the top, placed her laptop on it, and clapped her hands, beaming.

"It was all worth it, to see you so happy," Mike said.

"It's good to have a bit of home here at last."

Chase crooned, "Reunited and it feels so good." Then, with hands on his hips, he said, "You know, there's still a trailer full of stuff out there."

Mike got himself a soda out of Laurie's fridge and began singing the refrain to Chase's song. "Well I'm a no one by day, but I'm a nabob in nighttown." The others joined in and finished the chorus as they walked down the stairs.

* * *

Laurie and Mike led the way to Mary's house in the blue truck while Chase followed in his own vehicle. "I really do appreciate you bringing my stuff down," Laurie said. "I know it's a hassle, pulling the trailer and all."

"Not a problem. I was hoping we could get together. Plus, you know I've been instructed to check on you and report back." Mike smiled and waggled his eyebrows. "You look like you're doing pretty well, all things considered."

" *What* things considered?"

"That you're starting your career over. That you're so far from the family, living in a state you only visited once before. That you're living alone for, like, the first time in your life. Dad thought you would have moved back home by now."

"Huh," Laurie grunted dismissively. Still, she knew Mike was right. Except for a brief time while her divorce was being finalized, she had scarcely ever lived on her own. She had gone from her parent's home to college where she roomed with Mary, a friend she had known for years. Then she got married and moved in with DB only a couple of months after graduation.

"Yeah, it has been different," she admitted. "I guess that's why I've stayed so busy volunteering at the Treasure Chest, and meeting with the writers group, and working on the extra articles for the paper. It keeps my mind off things. I do love calling my own shots, and I don't mind working on my own, on articles and stuff. You have to be self-motivated, or life as a 'creative entrepreneur' doesn't work out." She thought for a while. "But it was disorienting, being suddenly single. It felt like free-falling – like being on a high wire without a safety net. But I'm doing okay."

"Well, I think you're doing more than okay," Mike said. "Just remember, there are people up north who love you. Don't be afraid to lean on us whenever you have to."

"Thanks, brother o' mine," she said, glad to hear it, but rolling her eyes nevertheless.

"I mean it! I'm pretty proud of you, and how independent you are these days. I've seen some of the articles you've sent to Dad. And there's a stubborn streak in you, in a good way. You're a strong person, and I'm sure you'll succeed at whatever you set your mind to."

Laurie felt herself blushing. "Turn here. This is Mary's street," was all she said.

Pete was out in the yard running a weed-eater when Mike backed the trailer into the driveway. Pete helped unload, but didn't look too happy about losing part of his garage to Laurie's furniture. Mary was enraptured by a child-size rocking chair, which Laurie said she could borrow for Ricky's room. "I remember this furniture," Mary said. "Was this all you kept from your house?"

"This stuff and the desk my grandma gave me. When DB and I broke up, he didn't want anything and neither did I, except for items that weren't associated with that marriage at all."

"But you had a set of china, and all that kitchen stuff."

"It was his mom's china. I didn't really want it, and I have no idea what he did it with it. Nor do I care. But I like my old bedroom stuff. It's really only half the set, though, because my sister kept her bed and dresser."

"And storing it here is just temporary, right?" Pete asked after he and Mike had the furniture snugged up against the wall.

"It's just temporary," Laurie said. "If I don't move into a house or a bigger apartment anytime soon, I'll get another storage unit down here." She deliberately did not look at Chase.

After working all afternoon, no one felt like cooking or even going to a restaurant. Chase made a run to a local barbecue place and brought back a couple of large carry-out bags. Mary put plates and silverware on the table, and pulled containers of pulled pork, barbecued ribs, baked beans, and Brunswick stew out of the bags.

"Mm-mm-mm." Mike wiped barbecue sauce off his face. "These ribs are the best. I might just have to move to Georgia."

"Come on down," Laurie told him.

"What do you think of Georgia so far?" Pete asked.

"It's hot! I can see why you guys have a swimming pool."

"Spring is my favorite," Mary said. "It goes on forever here. One thing blooms after another."

"I'm sure I'll be back, if you end up staying in Georgia," Mike said, looking at Laurie. "Which I hope you do, after I dragged all your stuff down here! Lisa said she wants to come visit too, maybe when it starts snowing up north." Lisa was Mike and Laurie's big sister.

"I know!" Mary said, "I'll get my sister to come down too. Then we could do a girl's thing – go to Savannah, or the beach, or something."

"That would be fun," Laurie agreed.

"Or maybe the whole family will come down." Mike wiggled his eyebrows. "Like for a wedding or something."

Laurie could feel her face starting to color. "Oh?" she asked innocently. "Have you gotten engaged to a Georgia Peach without telling me? Why are you really down here, Mike? It's not really a convention, is it."

Mike smiled, but everyone was looking at Laurie and Chase, and Laurie's blush deepened.

"Hey, we'll be happy to oblige," Chase said, coming to her rescue. "When's a good time for y'all? When does the snow really set in up there?"

"Oh, January or February are usually pretty good times *not* to be in Ohio," Mike said.

"Well, we'll try to work something out. Now who wants this last rib? Speak now, or it's mine."

Mike checked his watch and asked Chase about traffic on the interstate as Chase and Laurie walked him outside. He gave Chase a firm handshake and a nod. Then he put his arm around Laurie's shoulder as the two walked over to the truck. Mike gave her a final hug, and whispered, "I like him, Laurie. He seems like a nice guy, and I hope things work out for the two of you."

"I hope so too," she said. *I hope so too.*

Chapter 21.

The following week started out busy at the *Journal.* Laurie was back to work on the events column, and with fall in full swing and Christmas a couple of months away, there were plenty of events to edit. Laurie didn't have to, but she often called whoever submitted them to get additional information. Sometimes the event sounded interesting enough for a full article, and Laurie was busier than ever with freelance work. It didn't leave her much time for working on her novel, but c'est la vie. At least she was doing plenty of writing.

At the top of the *Journal's* event list was the city's Halloween celebration set for Saturday evening. Many of the downtown merchants planned to stay open late and give out candy and treats or hold special sales. There would be a costume contest, and live music on the lawn of the courthouse. Laurie texted a note to Chase about it, and he quickly texted back:

Already planning to take you

Laurie spent the rest of the day chasing down information about "Christmas in Chinkapin," an annual week-long extravaganza, and got all kinds of ideas which she weaved into an essay about Christmas that evening.

By Tuesday she was ready for something different, though. After work and lunch she stopped in at the Treasure Chest to help out for a couple of hours, and to catch up with Mary. She said a quick hello to Virginia, who was working at the front desk, and went looking for Mary in the back of the store.

"I hoped I'd find you here," Laurie said. Mary was in the sorting room, with a stack of newly-tagged clothes on the table in front of her.

"Here, you want to put these on hangers?" she said, indicating the blouses. "I'll do the pants. So how was work today?"

Laurie told her briefly about her day, and then switched topics. "It was sure nice seeing Mike Sunday."

"It was," Mary agreed. "A taste of home. It looked like he and Chase got along pretty well. Did Mike say anything about him?"

"Yeah, he said he liked Chase, and hoped things went okay for us. Well, you heard him, practically asking when the wedding was set for." Laurie stroked the base of her bare ring finger with her left thumb. She wanted to ask Mary what she thought about the fact that Chase hadn't proposed, or anything. Of course, *she* could do the proposing. If only she was more nervy about matters of the heart.

She knew Mary would have plenty of suggestions for what Laurie *should* do, and decided not to open herself up for that. "I think Mike's pushing things," she said finally. "We don't need to rush into anything. Chase and I did have a nice time Saturday, though. Have you ever been to Springwood Gardens, over by Peach Valley?" Laurie launched into a description of the gardens.

"We almost never go out that way," Mary said. "Sounds like I'll have to put it on my list of places to go. I hope to be getting out more with Ricky in the stroller in the next few months."

"Hey, how would you like to ride up to Atlanta with me?"

"I'd love to go to Atlanta. I need to do some shopping. I'm sure Pete wouldn't mind looking after Ricky for the day."

"I wasn't talking about shopping, actually," Laurie said. "I want to go to the Margaret Mitchell House, just to check it out. Plus maybe they can tell us what that book in our file cabinet is worth. I was thinking of going Friday, if I can get off work a little early."

"Oh! We really should see it. Pete will be at work, but I guess we could take Ricky with us, if I feed him before we leave. And we could go to one of the wonderful cafes in Atlanta. You think we can get up there and back without getting caught in rush-hour traffic?"

"Um. I hope so? I don't know. You've lived in Georgia longer than I have."

"Well, let's try it."

Virginia joined them in the sorting room. "It has been a slow afternoon," she said, examining the clothes hanging on the rack along one side of the room. "I think we can put some more of these long sleeved blouses and sweaters out, don't you?"

"Is it getting a little thin up front?" Laurie asked. "I didn't even stop to look."

"Well, they won't sell if they're hanging back here," Virginia said. "And we have been selling a lot of sweaters lately. By the way, your phone was making noises a minute ago."

The women loaded their arms with items appropriate to the season, and carried them to the front of the store. As the others hung up the clothes, Laurie

Finders Keepers

stopped in the office to check her phone. She was surprised to see she'd missed a call from Luke.

She listened to his brief message asking her to give him a call back, but decided to put it off for later. She couldn't imagine what it was about. Laurie still wondered what the story was between him and his helper, Cory, or whatever her name was. Maybe Luke was a player – a womanizer. She decided Luke could wait for her to call him back.

The bells on the door jangled, and Mary exchanged a surprised look with Virginia. "Hi, Alice," Mary said. "How are you doing?"

"I'd be better if I could find my wallet. I believe I left it somewhere. Have you seen it?"

"Your wallet? I don't think so. When did you even work here? I mean, how long ago did you miss it?"

Alice walked around the counter into the office. The handbag slung over her arm did look lighter than usual. "I worked one day last week," she said. She sounded confused.

"I hope we didn't put it out for sale," Laurie said with a smile. "Tell us what your wallet looks like."

"It's leather, I think, and it has a zipper in it. Oh, you know...it looks like a wallet! Just a regular wallet." She was getting agitated.

"Hmmm. That's not much to go on," Laurie said, looking at Mary.

"Come and sit down," Virginia said, leading Alice to one of the office chairs, and sitting down herself. "I think you need to just catch your breath, and then maybe you'll remember where you saw it last. Did you buy something the last time you were here?"

All the women who worked at the Treasure Chest were good customers. Mother Barbara often quipped about the fact that on any given Sunday she knew at least a few of the parishioners were clothed in outfits put together from Treasure Chest donations.

Alice sat for a moment, but didn't seem any more relaxed. "Don is going to be mad at me, if I've lost my credit cards and everything. But I don't know where I could have put my wallet." She looked around the office helplessly.

The shop phone rang, and Laurie answered it, surprised to hear Don's voice on the phone asking if Alice was there.

"Yes, she is," Laurie said, glancing back toward the woman in question. "She's here looking for her wallet. She thought she might have left it."

Laurie heard Don sigh. "I didn't even realize she had left the house until I saw the car was gone out of the driveway. She misplaced that wallet in the house yesterday. Didn't really misplace it, she just set it on the dresser, and then when it wasn't in her purse this afternoon she got upset. But it's still here on the dresser."

"Well, that's good news. She was worried about losing her credit cards."

"Would you tell her I have it here, and send her on home, please? Her daughter and I are trying to plan supper," he said.

"I sure will. Take care." Laurie ended the call and walked back to the office. "Alice? That was Don. He said your wallet is at home on your dresser."

Alice wore a look of puzzled amazement. "Well, what is it doing on my dresser?"

Laurie shrugged, holding her hands palm up, and shook her head. "He asked me to send you on home."

"I guess I'd better go on home, then, if Don said so. Are you girls sure you don't need my help today?" Alice asked the question as if that had been her sole reason for coming to the thrift shop.

"No, we're fine, the three of us," Virginia told her. "You can go on home. We'll see you next Tuesday."

"All right then, I'll leave you to it," Alice said with a bright smile. "And I'm so glad I found my wallet!"

"You saved yourself a lot of hassle," Laurie agreed.

Alice strolled out of the office with a smile and a wave. "Bless her heart," Virginia said. "She's getting more forgetful by the day." She turned to watch out the window a moment as Alice backed her car out of the parking space and disappeared down the road.

Chapter 22.

The next day Laurie saved the files on her laptop and was tidying her desk to leave the *Journal* office when her phone rang. Luke's name popped up on the screen, and immediately she remembered his message from the previous day.

"Hi, Luke." She made her voice sound extra cheerful. "I got your message yesterday, but didn't have a chance to call you. How's your bookstore doing?"

"Great. We've been so busy we've been able to hire another helper. I've got two additional employees now, students at the college. That works well because it brings in some of the other college folk. Which brings me to what I was calling about. The professor I mentioned, Cory Abrams, is definitely interested in taking a look at that first edition you all have. Is it still at the thrift shop?"

"Yes it is. We've kept it wrapped up and stashed in the file cabinet."

"Well, I told her I would pass her information to you, and you could give her a call and set up a time for her to see it." Laurie grabbed a pen and paper as Luke rattled off the info.

As Laurie wrote the professor's name down, a little lightbulb lit up over her head. "Cory. That's not the person who was helping you stock shelves the day I visited you at the bookstore, is it?"

"Yes, that's her. She didn't have any teaching that day, so she offered to help me." Laurie waited a moment to see if Luke had anything else to add but he remained silent. *Even more interesting,* she thought.

"Okay," she said finally. "Thanks again for thinking of us. We'd love to learn whether the book is valuable, and then hopefully find a buyer for it. It deserves to be somewhere better than the bottom drawer of a file cabinet. I'll give Cory a call today."

Laurie placed the call before something else could distract her. There was no answer, so she left a voice mail, and then drove home for something to eat.

She spent that afternoon in her apartment working on an essay. There were always writing contests she wanted to enter, but she never had much luck trying to come up with something on the spot that met their themes. It was better for her to work on essays or stories as the ideas came to her. Then when a contest was announced, if she had something "in the can" that filled the bill she could send it off. Once every couple of weeks she looked at upcoming contests and considered whether she had anything to send, but today was a writing day.

Late in the afternoon her phone rang. She had just been thinking about Chase and supper, so she swiped across the screen without really looking. "Hello, gorgeous. Are you cooking up something nice for me?" she asked.

There was no answer.

"Hello?" Laurie pulled the phone away from her ear and looked at the screen. It was the professor, Cory Abrams. Laurie heard a voice speaking over the phone, and quickly put it back to her ear.

"Hello. This is Cory Abrams from Peach Valley State, calling to speak to Laurie Lanton. Is this Laurie?"

"Yes! I'm so sorry, I thought you were...someone else. Yes. Thanks for calling me back!" Laurie was glad she couldn't blush over the phone. It was embarrassing enough as it was.

Cory joked that she didn't mind being called gorgeous, and apologized to Laurie that she wasn't cooking up anything at the moment, though she did love to bake. She had a warm voice, and Laurie appreciated her sense of humor. Then Cory mentioned a little about her credentials, and asked a few questions about the condition of the Treasure Chest's old copy of *Gone With the Wind*.

"I don't know the first thing about old or rare books," Laurie admitted, "so I don't even know what you would look for. I could bring it to Peach Valley. Or if you're heading to Chinkapin any time soon, maybe you could drop by the Treasure Chest." She told Cory the store's hours.

"Actually, I did want to see your shop. Tomorrow will work out great for me, because I have some other business in Chinkapin. What time can I meet you there?"

"We're open from ten o'clock 'til four. I work a morning job elsewhere. I should be at the shop around one, though, and I'd love to talk to you to learn more about all this."

* * *

Thursday morning thoughts of meeting the professor popped intermittently into Laurie's head. She herself had almost majored in literature at school, but at the last minute she had switched to communications and marketing, thinking it would improve her job prospects. She could always write the great American novel in her spare time, and then quit her job after she became rich and famous. The memory brought a smile to her lips. It was a good thing she was thrifty, because getting rich was taking longer than it was supposed to.

She finished her shift at the *Journal*, stopped at home for a quick lunch, and then zoomed over to the thrift shop. The bells on the door jangled as she walked in.

Carol glanced out of the office where she was sorting through a box of Christmas items, putting price tags on things in preparation for when they would set up their "Christmas room."

"How's it going?" Laurie asked. "Busy today?"

"Not bad for a Thursday. You should see the beautiful manger set I just pulled out of this box. Come take a look."

Laurie entered the office and stashed her purse. On top of the desk was a beautiful miniature stable with the usual animals and at least a dozen colorful-ly-painted figurines, including the holy family, wise men, shepherds and several angels. "That is a beauty. I wonder why someone got rid of such a nice nativity scene. I bet it'll sell fast."

"I think so too," Carol said. "We don't seem to have many Christmas items to start with this year. But, you know, as people get to decorating they bring stuff in. In another month or so we'll get a lot more."

Joan appeared from one of the back rooms and dumped an armload of nightgowns and robes on the counter. "Well hello, Laurie. I didn't expect to see you today," she said. "There are a million winter clothes that need tagging in the back. You might want to escape while you have a chance."

"I'm meeting someone here this afternoon: Cory Abrams. She's a literature professor at the college in Peach Valley. She's going to take a look at our *Gone With the Wind*. It's still in the file cabinet, isn't it?" Laurie suddenly felt the urge to check. She yanked open the bottom drawer of the cabinet, but the book was right where she'd seen it last. "Thank God. I was afraid Evelyn had made it disappear like she made off with that pocket watch that time."

"I hope this professor knows what the book is worth," Carol said. "Otherwise I don't know what we'll do with it."

"I tried looking online, but there are so many books out there, with such a range of prices," Laurie said. "I thought we might sell it on eBay or something, but I wouldn't have a clue what to ask for it."

"If she wants to buy it, tell her we have a lot more where that came from. Not signed, but there are a bunch of old books Evelyn has been saving. They're in that box under the worktable." Carol pointed. "Evelyn keeps saying she's checking on what they're worth, but they've been just sitting there for ages."

The bells on the door jangled and a curvy, dark-haired woman walked up to the counter where Joan was still standing. "Good afternoon. My name is Cory Abrams. I'm looking for Laurie Lanton."

It was definitely the woman Laurie had seen at the bookstore, although she hadn't seen much more than her head above the shelves. "Hi. I'm Laurie. Glad to meet you. Or meet you again, I guess." Laurie came out of the office and walked around the counter to shake hands. Cory wore a short, natural hairstyle, and was attractively dressed in a belted sweater over a narrow skirt. "Would you like to look around for a minute or do you want to see 'the book'?'" Laurie asked, raising her eyebrows with a smile.

"I'm really interested in seeing the book you have. I think I'll save the shopping for afterward."

Laurie led her into the office, and offered her a chair. She brought the book out of the file cabinet and laid it on the worktable. Joan had gone back to tag more clothes, but Carol and Laurie looked on as Cory examined the book for what seemed like forever. Finally Laurie couldn't wait any longer.

"What can you tell us about it?"

"This is a great book."

Carol's face lit with excitement. "All right!" she said, raising her hand to give Laurie a high five.

Cory looked at the two women, shaking her head. "I mean *Gone With the Wind*. It's a great work of fiction, and distinctly American. But I hope you won't be too disappointed when I tell you this particular copy is *not* worth a fortune. For one thing, it's actually the second printing of the first edition. The first batch were printed with a date of May, 1936, even though the book actually came out in June. You see?" She pointed to the June date on the copyright page.

"So this copy is actually the second printing?" Laurie asked.

"Exactly right. This information is available on the internet, so anyone could determine that much." Cory glanced at them again, and Laurie shrunk a bit.

She prided herself on her research skills, but this time she must have missed something.

"I take it there was no dust jacket with the book?" Cory asked.

Carol shook her head. "It was at the bottom of a box with a bunch of other things someone donated. The box was just left outside the door." She turned to Laurie. "Mary and I showed it to you the day after we got it."

Laurie nodded.

"Let me tell you a little about how we evaluate books." Cory launched into "instructor" mode. "See how the corners and the ends of the spine are rubbed and bumped? Almost a bit frayed-looking? And if you look at the edges of the pages with the book closed, do you see how they are a bit stained? And the pages are foxed."

"Foxed? What does foxed mean?" Laurie asked.

"That's what they call the rusty-looking reddish-brown patches and spots. You find this a lot in old books. The spots are sometimes caused by mildew or exposure to moisture." She examined the outside of the book. "The spine has some definite creases in it, and looks a little faded or bleached. They call that 'sunned.' It's just faded from being exposed to the sun, or to UV rays in general. Maybe it was on a book shelf in a sunny room. You can see the front and back covers are not as faded, so it must have stood between other books."

"So a dust jacket protects from more than just dust," Carol said.

"Uh-huh. The spine usually is the worst on an old book like this, but here – you can see the tops of the boards are faded too."

Cory opened and closed the book a few times, and leafed through the pages. "The front hinge is weak. Some of the pages are a bit creased." Finally she turned to the inscription inside. She leaned closer for a better look and then laughed out loud. "Oh, I'm sorry, but this just looks like a fake. Here. I've got some photos of Mitchell's authentic autograph." She set the book down and pulled her phone out of her purse. After searching a moment she showed the women an image. "Take a look at this."

Carol squinted at the screen and then looked at the book. "They look the same to me."

"But look here," Cory pointed. "See in the book where it looks like the signature is interrupted, like the signer lifted the pen, or paused while they were writing? And the same thing again here. Not in the dedication, where Joseph Barnes's name is written, but just on Margaret's signature. Someone tried to make this look real by copying an actual signature, but when people do that they'll pause to check the original and then continue writing. That's what happened here. Plus if this were original from the 1930's the ink would be oxidized. Faded. Have you ever seen an old letter or document, and the ink looks brown rather than black?"

"Oh, right!" Carol said. "I have some old family letters, and the ink does look brown."

"I'm starting to think someone tried to pass this book off as the real deal, and when they couldn't they just dumped it here," Laurie said.

Cory nodded. "Probably tried to sell it somewhere and was laughed out of the store. Or tried to sell it online maybe, but...." She shook her head. "Buyer beware. Most rare book collectors know what they're dealing with."

"Well this has been interesting," Laurie said. "You've taught us a lot. We're so glad you took the trouble to come see us." She was already thinking about writing an article about Professor Cory Abrams and her interesting sideline. It might make a good feature story.

"Not a problem. I had to bring my dress to the seamstress here in Chinkapin for a few alterations, so I was coming anyway."

"Is it a wedding dress?" Carol asked.

"It is. Well, probably not like you're thinking. This is my second wedding, so it's a tea-length dress. Ivory. In fact, I found it in a thrift shop in Redding! I think it's beautiful, but I need a little more room in the bust." She smiled, and suddenly looked shy and girlish.

"So when's the wedding?" Carol asked.

"Just before Christmas. It's going to be at St. Michael and All Angels. Maybe Luke told you." She looked to Laurie for confirmation.

"Luke!" *So much for wondering about him being a womanizer*, Laurie thought. She would have guessed Cory was a few years older than Luke, not that it mattered. Then again, she never was a very good judge. She remembered the strands of gray in Luke's beard, and the wrinkles around his eyes.

Cory seemed to be expecting some additional comment from Laurie. "How exciting. I had no idea." Maybe Laurie would wait a while to ask Cory for an interview about old books, and give the woman a chance to forget what a dullard she was.

Cory went on. "Yes, we're getting married. A lot of things have fallen in place for us in the last few months. Luke just bought a house in Peach Valley, the house his grandparents used to own. And we were able to get the money together for the bookstore franchise."

Laurie nodded, remembering that Luke had mentioned a silent partner who provided financing for the bookstore, while he was the cheap labor. A lot of things were making sense, in an odd sort of way. "When I interviewed Luke we just talked about the bookstore, and Peach Valley."

"It was a nice article," Cory said. "The publicity has definitely helped the store get off to a good start."

"Glad to hear it. As an aspiring novelist, I'm mighty fond of bookstores." *And that sounded lame*, Laurie thought.

"Luke told me you were a writer. He wanted me to go to the writers group meeting that Saturday, but I had student essays to grade. I'd be interested in seeing some of your fiction, if you ever want a beta reader. You know, Luke and I met when he was looking for a critique partner years ago. He got a little more than he bargained for." Cory smiled, and her eyes twinkled. "Anyway, I just have a few more minutes, so let me browse around the shop and see what you have."

"Of course," Laurie said. She pointed out where to find various merchandise in the store. As Cory walked off, Laurie said quietly "A little disappointing about our book."

"Oh, well, we can't expect to find hidden treasure in every box that shows up on our doorstep," Carol said.

"We've learned something about old books, anyway. Let's pull out these other books Evelyn has set aside, and get Cory to take a look before she leaves. Otherwise, we might as well start donating more of our books to the Friends of the Library."

A customer entered the shop with her daughter in tow. Laurie showed the mother some items in the jewelry case while the girl looked at purses. Carol went to help Joan hang clothes. Several minutes later Cory came back to the front counter with an armload of books.

"Did you find something you can use?" Laurie said, surprised.

"You had a lot of good books back there! All these are options in my American Lit class. My students have to select a book from the list for their final project. I thought I'd pick these up here and offer them to the kids so they don't have to spend any more money than they already do. As long as you don't tell Luke I'm buying books at a thrift shop, and not at Franklin's! So what do you charge for your books?"

"Oh, just take them," Laurie said. "Payment for services rendered, if I can get you to glance at this other stack of books here."

Cory quickly looked through the old books Evelyn had set aside. As Laurie suspected, none of them was especially valuable.

"Are you sure you don't want me to pay for these? I don't mind," Cory said.

"Absolutely," Laurie assured her. "Everything in the shop was donated to us, and one of the reasons we're here is to give back to the community. We'd be happy to know students will be using these. Here, I'll even put them in a bag for you." She rummaged under the counter and found a cloth tote bag. "This will make them easier to carry."

"This is wonderful. I really do appreciate it."

"No problem. Thanks for the education about old books," Laurie said. "Maybe I can call you sometime if I have more questions."

"Absolutely. You ladies have a good afternoon."

A few more customers came into the shop, and in between Laurie and Carol tagged items. At closing time Laurie went to grab her purse and cell phone, and tidy up the office. She tossed a few things in the top drawer of the file cabinet and paused with her hand on the stack of old books.

"What are we going to do with those," Carol asked, "put the old books out to sell, or donate them to the 'Friends'?"

"I was just thinking some of what Cory talked about would make an interesting feature article. I might save *Gone With the Wind* and a couple of these other old books to use for illustrations. You know, photos of where they're 'foxed' and everything. And maybe talk about the forged signature."

"That would be interesting. And you could mention the Treasure Chest in your article, and give us some free publicity."

"Free publicity is always good," Laurie agreed. "Speaking of which, I was thinking of putting an ad on our Facebook page. What do you think about a half-price sale on books?"

"Go for it," Carol said, and hit the total key on the calculator. "Just don't tell Evelyn I said it was okay."

Chapter 23.

"OMG this is *awful*," Laurie exclaimed, hitting the brakes again as traffic on I-75 slowed to a crawl. She and Mary had gone to Atlanta to visit the Margaret Mitchell House in Midtown, and were driving home in the middle of rush hour. "I wish there was another way to get home. I told you we should have left sooner."

"You told me no such thing, you little fibber," Mary said. "You dragged me into that café with that glazed 'I-need-coffee' look in your eyes, and when you saw scones in the pastry case wild horses could not have pulled you out. Plus I needed to feed Ricky."

"I *hate* rush hour traffic," Laurie growled again as someone from the next lane squeezed into the three-inch gap she had left between herself and the car in front of her.

"I guess every now and then I need to remind myself why I don't drive to Atlanta very often," Mary agreed. "Remember when Ricky was born, and Pete had to drive home from here? I don't know how he made it back to Chinkapin as quick as he did."

"He must have been flying. Thank God Roly's been asleep for the last hour."

"Don't look now, but I think he's starting to wake up." Mary sat catty-corner facing Ricky's car seat in the back.

"Quit looking. He can probably feel your eyes on him."

"So when are you coming over for movie marathon? I really want to see the movie again now." Seeing everything about the December, 1939, movie premiere of *Gone With the Wind* in Atlanta had piqued Mary's interest.

"We haven't done that in a while. It might be fun. Come to think of it, the last time I came to your house to watch a movie was the night before Roly was born."

"Well, I'm not pregnant, so now might be a good time." A smile broke out on Mary's face. "Hi, there, sweet pea. Are you awake?" She reached into the back seat to tweak the baby's foot, and then grabbed her phone and snapped a quick picture.

After a few minutes Laurie rolled down her window a couple of inches. "Phew! Mary, it's getting a little stinky in here." She wrinkled her nose and glanced in the rear view mirror at the car seat in the back.

"Yeah. I was afraid of that. Especially after he ate so much."

"Do I need to find a place to pull over?"

"Pull over, nothin'. It would take too long to get to the next exit. And you know there are barely any rest areas on this interstate." She slid her seat back as far as it would go.

"What are you doing?" Laurie's eyes darted back and forth between the rear-view mirror and the road in front of her.

"Taking care of business, girlfriend. I've done this before, and I'm going to do it again." Mary unbuckled her seatbelt, turned around to kneel in her seat, and leaned over the back of it. She rummaged in the diaper bag and spread a changing mat on the seat behind her.

"This has got to fall under the heading of 'distracted driving,'" Laurie said.

"Just keep your eyes on the road. I'll handle this." Mary lifted the baby out of his car seat and laid him on the mat. "Oof! This can't be good for my back." She kept up a patter with the baby, who was being pretty quiet, all things considered.

"Thank God for electric windows in cars! What did people do when they had to crank them all down?" Laurie opened the other windows a crack to let in some fresh air – at least, as fresh as it got on the interstate. She kept her eyes on the road as Mary finished up in the back seat. "I hope you have a plastic bag to put that thing in. Or maybe we should just throw it out the window at that guy who's been on my tail for the last ten miles."

With another groan Mary lifted Ricky and secured him in his car seat. She turned back around, slid her seat forward, and buckled up. "There. All done."

"That was pretty impressive! I didn't think you could do it," Laurie said.

"I've been training to be on one of those ninja warrior TV shows. Seriously, I have been doing some yoga."

"Ooh! With goats? Goat yoga?"

"With goats!" Mary snorted. "Heck no. I'm paying for this class. Let the goats get fit on their own dime."

"Seems like you're getting used to this motherhood thing." In the mirror Laurie could see Ricky contentedly gnawing on a stuffed rabbit and looking out the window at the trucks passing by.

"Ricky's getting me trained, that's all. Pete is the one who has surprised me. I knew he'd be a good dad, but he's really spending a lot of time with Ricky, including changing diapers. When he's home, that is. But he's also the one to give Ricky a bath, which gives me some time to do things in the evening. And you should see the two of them reading together. It's adorable."

I wish I could get the hang of my life, Laurie thought.

Mary seemed to read her mind, because the next thing out of her mouth was, "How are things with you and Chase?"

"Hmmm," Laurie wondered how to answer.

"You have to think about it, huh?"

"You know, I've known him less than a year," Laurie said finally. "So why do I feel so anxious that we're not engaged yet?"

"I guess it depends on exactly *why* you want to be engaged. Have you thought about that? Is it for financial reasons?"

"Not really. I mean, I could rock along like I have been in that little apartment for a while, especially since the court ordered DB to provide me with health insurance. I'm handling my other bills okay."

"Well, have you talked to Chase about it? He's not a mind-reader, you know. You can't assume the two of you are on the same page. I mean, I don't think he's playing around or anything, but that doesn't mean a guy's ready for marriage. You told me his late wife was a real doozy. Honestly, he's probably scarred by what happened with her." Laurie had told Mary about Chase's late wife's drug use and death, and how Chase had lost everything because of it and had to reinvent his life.

Mary continued. "Plus, why marriage? I mean, how do you think that will change the relationship you have? Is there something more you're looking for? Besides a house, I mean. Because you could buy a house yourself, if you made it a goal, and cranked out more freelance articles..." Mary paused, and seemed to calculate for a moment. "Well, maybe not." She smiled.

"Stop laughing at me, Mary, this is serious." Laurie was smiling too. It was clear she wasn't going to get rich from her writing any time soon.

"Think of it from his perspective. What does marriage mean to Chase? What did it mean last time? A wife he couldn't trust, and heartache, and...."

Laurie interrupted "And giving up his dream career and losing everything. Yeah, I see what you mean."

"Which is the same thing that happened to you, if you think about it. You gave up a lot of your *self* to stay married to DB. Now you're at least doing the kind of creative work you always wanted. But since we're talking about careers, are you sure he's given up his dream of fame and the music business and all that? Maybe he still has that at the back of his mind. How would you feel about it?"

"Oh, I don't think he'd be working so hard at the HVAC business if he wasn't serious about staying here," Laurie said. "Would he?"

"Well, he has had a couple of his songs recorded. I'm just saying. And what are you thinking about in terms of a second wedding? Did Chase and whatever-her-name-was have a big elaborate wedding in front of God and everybody? Maybe he's afraid that's what you want, you romantic little thing you. Maybe he can't face the idea of *that* all over again."

Mary paused, but her imagination was clearly on a roll. "Or maybe he's just trying to come up with a novel way to 'pop the question.' You know, people propose up in hot air balloons and...and, I don't know. What do you want?" Mary looked at Laurie, and waited for an answer.

"What do I want? I've been so much just wanting to be engaged. You know, the security of knowing Chase will be around."

"Yeah, but you were *married* to DB, and look how secure that was. It didn't stop him from playing the field with Miss Fancy Pants. *And* probably others. So why are you so eager to get married again?"

"I don't know. *I don't know!*" Laurie was feeling frustrated. "I guess I'm just insecure. I guess I just want to feel.... I want to feel loveable. Like I'm worth being married to, worth someone making a commitment to."

"Ooh, Laurie, you can't tie your self-worth to what other people think of you! That'll just drive you crazy. You're still hurt because of what DB did to you. Until that heals you *do not* need to rush into a marriage with anyone just because they say they love you. That's the way to wind up with the wrong partner and make yourself really unhappy. Besides, you *are* loveable. I love you. Your family loves you. And haven't you been paying attention in church? You are loved! The kind of love you can't buy, you can't earn, you don't deserve, but you're loved anyway. The kind of love that lasts forever and you can't shake off, like...like cat hair on your favorite sweater." The two burst out laughing. Laurie kept one hand on the steering wheel and wiped at her eyes with the other.

"You know me," Mary said. "I'm always free with my advice and my opinions, and I call it like I see it. I like Chase. Obviously I don't know him like you do, but I think he's a good guy. I think he's been hurt before and he's taking things slow. And that's just what you should do. Take things slow. Enjoy whatever it is you and Chase have together. But don't push it. Like you said, you haven't even known him for a year."

"You're right," Laurie said, "much as I hate to admit it." She smiled at Mary. "I'm just going to relax and enjoy life for a while. And I'm really going to enjoy that this traffic is finally letting up." She pressed her foot on the accelerator and cruised smoothly down the highway.

Chapter 24.

"It was an interesting place. You should see it some-time." Laurie sat at the kitchen table in Chase's apartment that evening and drank a glass of iced tea as she told him about her visit to the Margaret Mitchell house. "Carol had already told us a bit about it, and I googled it, so I knew it was basically a little in-town apartment building. It's a good thing, be-cause before that I had assumed it would be a planta-tion house!"

"You would have been pretty disappointed," Chase said, his head in the fridge. He pulled out some sandwich materials and set them on the counter.

"Yeah. She used to call it 'the dump.' It was amaz-ing to me how small the place was. Makes me feel better about these apartments we have. In fact, the kitchens here are bigger, and the bathrooms." She swirled the ice in her glass and took another drink. "She and her husband – her second husband, that is – just had a small ground-floor apartment, but the museum takes up the whole building. Part of the museum has exhibits about the making of the *Gone With the Wind* movie, and the big movie premier in Atlanta. Mary was really interested in that stuff. I was more interested in the information about Margaret herself – Peggy, I should say – and her journalism career. She was an interesting character: sort of counter-cultural, and ahead of her time. It was just tragic the way she died."

"Hit by a log truck or something, wasn't she?"

"Not a log truck, a car!" Laurie laughed, but then turned serious. "Actually, it was a taxi, driven by a drunk driver."

"That's pretty horrible," Chase said. He put together his sandwich and brought it to the table.

"Yeah. She didn't have it easy, I guess. That first husband of hers was really a schmuck. Worse even than DB."

"You're well rid of that dirtbag."

"I'm sorry Mary and I didn't get home sooner. It's just a long drive up there. By the way, we heard Trey McGann singing 'Climbin' the Walls' on the radio."

Chase laughed. "That's crazy."

"Anyway, the southbound traffic was really bad. I don't think starting home sooner would have made any difference. We just had to ride it out. Lucky for us Roly behaved most of the time. Otherwise it would have been awful."

"No worries, sugar." He kissed Laurie on the cheek. "It gave me a chance to catch up on paperwork. The office ladies and I were crunching numbers this afternoon, and then I was on the phone with Old Man Anderson in Florida."

"Yeah, I was surprised when you said you just got home."

"I want to show you something. Check this out." He retrieved a single page of a spreadsheet that lay on the coffee table in the living room, and handed it to Laurie. There was a curious expression on his face, almost like he was trying not to laugh.

"What am I looking at," she said, scanning the columns and trying to make sense of them.

"That shows where I've been paying off the Old Man for the business." Chase smiled, and took a big bite from his sandwich. He watched her face as she looked from him to the spreadsheet.

"But this says.... Oh!" Laurie's eyes widened as she finally understood. "Chase, it's all paid for! The business is yours!"

"Yes, ma'am. You are looking at the sole proprietor of Anderson HVAC."

"Woo-hoo!" Laurie bounced in her chair, and gave Chase a high-five. "Where's the champagne? You should be celebrating with a steak, not a sandwich!"

"I figured we'd plan the celebration together. Actually, I'd like to do something that involves the employees too. It's not exactly a one-man show."

"Yeah, you do have a good crew."

Chase finished his sandwich as the two discussed plans for an early "thanksgiving" luncheon at his workplace to celebrate the change in ownership. Finally he carried his plate to the sink and stretched. "I have got to take a shower and think about turning in. Today was a long day, and we both have to be up early."

A few minutes later Laurie heard the shower turn on. Chase cracked open the bathroom door to let some of the steam out, and she admired his bare back-side. His cell phone rang and he stuck his head out the door. "Can you get that, or see who it is?" he asked. "If it's important I'll call them when I get out." He disappeared back into the bathroom.

Laurie picked up his phone from the table and read the display. *Charlotte*, it said. She had no idea who Charlotte was. Laurie tried to remember the names of the two women who worked in Chase's office. She was pretty sure neither one was a Charlotte. Impulsively she answered the phone.

"Hello?"

"Oh," a woman's voice said, and there was a pause. "I was trying to reach Chase. Is this his number?"

"This is his phone. I'm Laurie, his *girlfriend*," she said, emphasizing the word. "He can't talk right now. Would you like to leave a message?"

"Well...." Charlotte hesitated. "Yes. I forgot to tell him something at the café this afternoon. Um...just ask him to call me. I guess it's not urgent. He uh.... Of course he has my number. I'm sorry, what did you say your name was?"

"*Laurie*," she enunciated, a little more loudly than necessary. "I'll give him the message."

"Thanks. Have a good night."

Without saying goodbye Laurie jabbed the screen to end the call. She sat staring at Chase's phone. *Something Charlotte forgot to tell Chase at the café that afternoon*, she thought. *Now isn't that interesting.*

Laurie conveniently "forgot" to give Chase the message. And if Charlotte called again Laurie missed it. She told herself it was probably nothing to worry about, but her mind wouldn't let it go. Various scenarios kept popping into her head. Maybe Chase was hiring another office worker, and had interviewed her at the café. Maybe Charlotte was an HVAC equipment supplier. Maybe she was a musician. Or maybe Charlotte was an old flame who was trying to wiggle her way back into Chase's life.

* * *

Chase was in a bubbly mood on Saturday. He and Laurie went to the packing shed for breakfast, and they arranged catering for a celebration party for his employees, to be held the following Friday.

It was to be a traditional Thanksgiving feast with turkey and all the trimmings, including both pumpkin and pecan pie. Chase said he would pick up all the food Friday morning and bring it to the warehouse. Laurie offered to come and help when she got off work, so the employees wouldn't get stuck with all the set-up and clearing away.

That afternoon when Chase led Laurie into his bedroom for a nap it seemed a waste of the glorious weather, since neither of them was drowsy. But sleep wasn't really on his mind. He pressed soft kisses on Laurie's lips, caressed her neck and shoulders, and then tugged her cotton shirt over her head.

Finders Keepers

She climbed on the bed and lay back against the pillows. As he kissed her she reached her hands up under his shirt, gently raking his back with her nails.

Before long their clothes were scattered on the floor and they had burrowed under the soft sheets. Warm skin met skin, and their kisses grew deeper as Chase's hands explored her body. He grazed her soft flesh with his lips, gradually moving lower.

Laurie clutched him moaning softly, and opened to him with a sigh, pressing against his touch until she convulsed in a prolonged ecstasy.

Disentangling himself from the sheets, Chase raised himself above her as she molded her body to his and pulled him closer. They kissed, moving together.

She opened her eyes again as he leaned up on his arms. She loved the sight of his powerful shoulders, enjoyed the feeling of strength and assurance as his body moved. She abandoned all thought, and pulled him to her, wrapping her arms tightly around his shoulders and nuzzling his neck as he pressed against her and buried his face in her hair.

He rolled onto his side, slipping one arm under her neck, and leaned his body against hers. They fell asleep, their legs and arms wrapped around each other, and dozed for nearly an hour.

The sound of a noisy muffler outside finally woke her, and Laurie found Chase gazing at her. He moved his head close and kissed her gently. "We're burning daylight," he said.

"I guess. But that was a lovely nap," she answered.

Neither moved for a moment, but finally Laurie's bladder wouldn't let her stay any longer. She slipped from the bed and padded into the bathroom. When she came back for her clothes, she was surprised to see Chase already in the living room, sitting on the couch with his guitar in hand.

He reached for the notebook he had been writing in, looked over his scribbling, and then started strumming and picking out a tune. Laurie listened for a moment, and recognized the mournful song he had been working on.

"Guess I'll let you work on your music for a bit while I go get some writing done."

He paused. "That sounds good. And then we'll...." He was obviously distracted. "We'll go into town for the Halloween thing."

"Yeah. I'll be back." She let herself out, softly closing the door.

* * *

Laurie sat at her computer and opened the document she had been working on, but couldn't focus on it. She was still thinking about that mournful, almost dirge-like tune Chase had been playing.

Impulsively, she googled "how to find a grave," and selected a website from the search results. A form popped up on her screen. She took a stab at filling in the blanks, guessing at most of it, and then clicked search.

She was dismayed by the results. So many people with the last name Harris! She scrolled down the screen clicking "next" several times to page through the results before she found what she was looking for.

There it was: Jennifer Renee Harris was buried in Evergreen Cemetery in Chinkapin, Georgia. She had died in the fall, just a little over a year ago. It had to be the right one.

Laurie sat pondering. Chase had seemed quieter than usual – with the exception of this morning. Could this be why? She hated to think he was still hung up on his late wife.

Maybe hung up was not the right word. After all, glad as Laurie was to be rid of her ex, she still thought about him from time to time, and still felt the effects of the years they had spent together.

She saved the website, and loaded the cemetery's address into her cell phone. It might just be time for a little field trip.

Chapter 25.

A couple of hours later Laurie texted Chase. Her stomach told her it was time to eat. She went down to his apartment and found him assembling ham sandwiches.

"Grab the coleslaw out of the fridge, would you?" he said.

"How come we don't just eat at the Halloween thing?" She looked from Chase to his guitar case standing by the door. "I thought we were going to the Coffee Pot and then checking out the rest of the action in town?"

"We are going to the Coffee Pot but I promised to play a short set there, so I want to eat first. They have live music tonight, and they specifically asked if I would play."

"What? But this was supposed to be our date!" Laurie gritted her teeth and growled.

"Hey, those people have been good to me. I felt kind of obligated to say yes. I told them to put me first so we would have time to stroll around and see everything." When Laurie didn't say anything, Chase came over and put his hands on her shoulders. "They asked me late last week. I figured you'd want to go downtown anyway. I'm sorry if I forgot to tell you. Guess I'm living too much inside my head."

"It's okay," she said, and sighed. "It'll be fun. You *will* buy me a latte, though, won't you?"

"They'll *give* you a latte, or I won't play." He kissed her on the lips. "But first, sandwiches." He went back to work.

Laurie fetched the coleslaw and some drinks, still grumbling about the slight change in plans. She knew Chase had played with a band in nightclubs and other venues, and that it used to be his dream to make it as a performer. She also knew that the long hours and late nights had been hard on his first marriage. There just weren't enough hours in the day for him to be a performer and run an HVAC business. So what was he thinking? She hoped this wasn't a sign of things to come. So much for her plan to relax and enjoy life!

She *tried* to relax. The people who owned the Coffee Pot *had* been good to Chase, as he said. Plus she loved hearing him play. She ruffled the back of his hair as he sliced the sandwiches in half, bringing a smile to his face.

Finders Keepers

As they ate Laurie remembered the call from the mysterious "Charlotte" the night before when Chase was in the shower and she'd picked up his phone. The woman had said she met Chase at the café. Maybe she had been the one who had talked him into playing tonight? Laurie certainly wasn't going to ask, since she hadn't bothered to tell him Charlotte called, or to give him the message. And Chase hadn't thought it was important enough to tell Laurie he had met Charlotte at the café, so – maybe it *wasn't* important. *Not everyone is as sneaky as DB*, she reminded herself.

The two were in town in minutes. Chase knew the back streets of Chinkapin, and found a parking place in a small lot behind a lawyer's office not far from the courthouse. Laurie looked around curiously. "I didn't know all these houses were back here," she said. "Where are we, anyway?"

"The Coffee Pot is just up here. Come on. I've only got a few minutes to set up." He grabbed his guitar case and strode quickly up the sidewalk, and Laurie followed.

On an outdoor stage on the other side of the courthouse a small country band was already playing. Through the music Laurie heard her phone ding, and checked it to find a message from Mary.

"Look." She held up her phone to show Chase an image of Pete and Mary, with Roly between them looking stunned. The baby was dressed in a pumpkin costume. "It looks like they're downtown somewhere." Laurie zoomed in to expand the picture. She texted a quick note and invited them to meet up with her at the cafe.

As Chase set up on the small stage at the café, Laurie ordered a pumpkin spice latte, a departure from her usual. Waiting for her drink, she saw Pete pull the door open, and helped Mary get the stroller over the door sill.

"Hi!" Laurie bent to take Roly's hand. "Aren't you a cute little pumpkin-baby!"

"We wanted to dress him in that Jack Skellington costume from the thrift shop, but it was too big," Mary said. "Maybe next year."

"What does he think about all this?"

"All the noise is a bit much," Pete said, "plus it's past his bedtime. Maybe Chase can play some lullabies for us, or at least something soothing." Pete hoisted the baby out of the stroller and went to greet Chase while Mary ordered a hot chocolate.

They grabbed a table near the stage as other people arrived and crowded around the counter. Acoustic guitar music flowed from the speakers, and then

Chase's voice, singing a melancholy song about falling leaves drifting by a window. Laurie savored the sweet, nostalgic music and sipped her coffee.

"You look like you could just stay here forever with that dreamy look on your face," Mary commented.

"I love the fall," Laurie said.

"I didn't mean the season. I meant Chase. You love to listen to him sing."

"Yeah, that too, but...."

"So what's the 'but'? I wish my husband had a cool hobby."

"If that's all it is," Laurie said, watching the other people in the café watching Chase.

"Oh, but you said-"

Laurie interrupted her. "Look, Mary, let's not talk about it now. I'm supposed to be out having a good time."

Mary raised her eyebrows. "Okay, then." She sat back in her chair, and they sipped their drinks in silence.

* * *

As soon as Chase's set ended Mary and Pete said their goodbyes and took the baby home. Chase packed up his guitar and placed it out of the way in a storage room backstage. "It'll be safe there for a while," he said to Laurie. "Let's go check out the action in town."

They strolled up the street looking at windows decorated for fall. They ducked in and out of shops, gathered a few pieces of candy to munch, and Chase commented on people's Halloween costumes. Laurie replied in monosyllables.

She clutched her paper cup which still held some of her latte, and remembered the first time she had gone to the Coffee Pot to hear Chase play. She glanced over at him, and saw him looking down. He pulled her aside out of the flow of pedestrians, wrapped his arms around her, and looked into her eyes. "Hey, Laura May. You're not going to let that latte come between us, are you?" He started to kiss her.

"No one comes between me and my latte," she said, lowering her head.

"Hey." He wrinkled his brow. "What's this about? What's the matter?"

"I'm just...tired, that's all. Maybe we should go home."

"Go home? I feel like we just got here. And we had that nap, so...." He looked around. Kids in costumes wearing glow-necklaces and light-up sneakers dodged in and out of the shops. Knots of people stood under the street lights talking and laughing. "Would you like to sit for a while? Maybe go listen to the band over by the courthouse?"

"No. Let's just go home. You know we have to get up early tomorrow."

Chase pulled the phone out of his pocket to glance at the time. "It's not that late. It's still thirty minutes until the costume contest." He looked at Laurie. Finally he shrugged. "Let's go back and get my guitar."

They turned and walked up the street in silence. Laurie drained the last of her coffee and pitched the cup in a bin in front of the café.

"The car's down that way." Chase led the way and the two walked in silence to the car, not holding hands.

Once inside the car Laurie couldn't stand it anymore. "Chase, I'm just worried that you're not ready to give up the music business. I wish you would have told me about this gig tonight."

"I don't see what the problem was. I played for twenty minutes while you visited with your friends."

She huffed. "It's not that. It's the songwriting, and-"

Chase cut her off. "Songwriting? What's wrong with that? What exactly do you want me to do while you're working on your articles and stuff? Sit there and watch you type?" He sounded exasperated.

"It's your mysterious meetings, and secret song deals," she said angrily.

"What are you talking about?" He glanced at her before looking back at the road.

"You know, all this mysterious stuff, and phone calls from *Charlotte*, and everything. What's that all about?"

As they waited for the traffic signal to turn green, Laurie looked at Chase's face in the glow of the street lights. He wore a pained expression: a look of recognition. *That struck a nerve*, Laurie thought. Her stomach sank.

"Look that's just...." Chase started and broke off. "There are some things I just can't...." He shook his head and let out a long breath. "Why are you picking a fight with me? There's nothing going on. I am not running off to Nashville. There's nothing to worry about." He sounded pleading, but then his tone changed. "If anything, you're the one meeting up with people and running around."

"Running around?" Her jaw dropped. "With who?"

"That guy with the funky mustache," Chase reminded her. "You met him up in Redding, you met him at that restaurant in Peach Valley.... Where else have you been meeting him?"

"Oh, for God's sake. You're just being stupid."

He pulled into the apartment parking lot and turned off the ignition. The two sat in silence until Laurie pulled open the car door and walked to the building without looking back. Chase followed her inside and watched as she dashed up the stairs to the third floor.

She barricaded herself behind her apartment door, threw down her bag, and paced around the room, her hands shaking. She wondered how much espresso they had put into her latte. Finally she picked up a pillow from the sofa and screamed into it.

Then she raised her head listening. Was that someone knocking? She heard it again. "Laurie?" Chase said through the door. "Let me in. Are you okay?"

"Go away," she said.

Chapter 26.

Laurie's phone rang early the next morning. She picked it up off the nightstand and looked at the screen. She let it ring several more times before finally answering.

"Hi," she said.

"Hey," Chase answered. There was a pause. "Are we riding together this morning?"

"Sure," she said.

"See you when you're ready, then." The screen cleared.

Laurie fell back on her pillows and closed her eyes. *I guess I'm on my own for breakfast*, she thought. Her hand went to her stomach. Actually she wasn't worried about breakfast. She was tired, and felt slightly nauseous. She told herself it was the coffee from last night, but a part of her knew that wasn't true.

Even living so close to St. Mark's it was sometimes a challenge getting there on time. The weather had turned a little cooler, and threatened rain. Laurie stared in her closet for a long time before choosing a simple A-line skirt in purple and shades of dark green. She paired it with a deep purple cashmere pullover that flattered her figure. She was almost at Chase's apartment and had to run up the stairs again to get a jacket.

Finally she knocked and opened his door. He got up from the kitchen table and set his coffee mug in the sink. "You look nice," he said, regarding her a moment before putting his hand on her shoulder and giving her a peck on the cheek. He looked into her eyes, but when she didn't respond he dropped his hand.

They drove to the church in silence. A few drops of rain pattered on the windshield, and yellow leaves skittered across the roadway. Chase parked in front of the Treasure Chest, and the two were half-way across the parking lot when Chase remembered a cable he had bought for the sound system. "Go on ahead. I'll catch up with you," he said, and dashed off to retrieve it from the car.

Laurie entered the narthex through the red double doors and shook the rain off her umbrella. It was early, and few people besides choir members were in the building. Everything was still. Laurie heard the whisper of pages turning in the loft, and imagined Steve leafing through music at the organ console.

She stepped into the nave and took a moment to admire the flower guild's handiwork. Two large, white bouquets flanked the shining brass cross that stood behind the altar. Another large cross was suspended from the ceiling.

The silence pressed against her ears. Suddenly there wasn't just air in the nave and sanctuary, but a presence filling the large space: something alive. Laurie strained to listen. *What?* she thought, and waited.

A phrase Mother Barbara occasionally used drifted through her mind: something about "living in the already and the not yet." She was never quite sure what that was supposed to mean. Something done and not yet done? Fulfilled, and still to come? She thought of the morning star that signaled approaching dawn, even when it was still dark outside.

Well, I'm waiting, she thought. Somewhere a door opened, and a cool breeze wafted into the nave, stirring a faint breath of Chase's after-shave, which clung to Laurie's hair from when he had kissed her that morning. In a brief flash she remembered their nap of the previous afternoon. Her body grew warm as she thought of the pleasures of their love-making. Then she shivered, and recalled their argument.

A mighty pedal note sounded from the organ in the loft above as Steve launched into the opening of *For All the Saints.* The door behind her opened, and Chase entered holding a long black cable. "I found it. Ready?" He had started toward the stairs to the loft, but turned and walked over to her. "What?" he said. "You look like you're waiting for something."

She shook her head. "Come on." They climbed the stairs into the loft.

Laurie squeezed past Mary to take a seat, and joined in the hymn. "Thank you, choir, that'll be fine," Steve said after the second verse. "Let's turn to hymn number 660."

Choir members flipped through their hymnals, placing ribbons to mark the day's selections, and Laurie greeted her friends. She had forgotten that today they were observing All Saints Day. A baptism was scheduled too. It looked like it would be a long service.

She fumbled with her bulletin, and a slip of paper fell out. Retrieving it, she saw it was an insert listing names of the recently departed who were to be remembered during the service. As Steve began to play, her eyes moved quickly down the alphabetical list until she found the name: Jennifer Renee Harris. Laurie glanced over at Chase, who was busy connecting the new cable to the sound system. Beside her Mary gave her a quizzical look and indicated her hymnal. Laurie stashed the page back in her bulletin, and joined in singing.

The baptism went smoothly. "The parents must have practiced dousing the baby at home," someone in the front row whispered. The little one never cried, but took everything in stride, and seemed to enjoy being paraded up and down the center aisle.

Finally one of the lay readers stood up to lead the prayers of the people, and read aloud the names of the departed listed in the bulletin insert. Laurie turned slightly as she listened, and glanced behind her just before Jennifer's name was called. Chase stood still, looking straight ahead. Laurie looked away a second, and then glanced back again. His head was bowed and his eyes were tightly closed.

Laurie faced forward feeling conflicted. She could only imagine what Chase had been through, losing someone dear to him and everything he owned in the process. But she was still angry at him.

Passing the peace took a little longer than usual. A few people gathered around the family with the new baby, and took the opportunity to greet visitors who were there for the baptism. In the loft there was the usual "grand left and right" as choir members hugged each other and waved to their friends below. Laurie looked over the balcony rail at the crowd below, and a question occurred to her.

Chase had stepped over to the other side of the loft to adjust something on the sound system. Laurie leaned toward Mary and casually asked, "Hey, do you know anyone in the parish named Charlotte?"

"Charlotte? Hmmm. I don't think so. Then again, you and I know most of the same people. They're either in the choir or they work at the Treasure Chest."

"Yeah, that's true."

Tracy, one of the sopranos, had overheard her question and turned around. "Alice has a daughter named Charlotte. She lives in Alabama, but she visits here every now and then."

Laurie nodded, but couldn't think why Alice's daughter would be contacting Chase about church music, or anything else for that matter. And Alice was an older woman. Any daughter of hers would probably be – well, at least older than the age Laurie had guessed for the woman she saw talking to Chase in the apartment parking lot. Not that Laurie actually got a good look at her. She fished for more information. "Is she blonde, maybe early thirties?"

Tracy snorted. "If she's thirty, she's been thirty for a long time."

Their conversation was interrupted as Mother Barbara made a few announcements, and the service resumed.

After the service Steve left quickly for a function in Redding, leaving choir members to join the coffee hour for a change. Having skipped breakfast, Laurie was famished, and followed the others to the kitchen, filling her plate with snacks from the offering arranged along the kitchen counter.

She got to the end of the line and Chase reached for her plate. "I'll carry these to the parish hall if you'll get us some coffee."

Laurie nodded. She noticed his plate was heaped with cheese and crackers and other snacks, and suspected he also had skipped breakfast. She turned toward the coffee pot where Evelyn was pouring herself a cup. "How are you this morning, Evelyn?" Laurie forced herself to sound cheerful.

"I need to talk to you." Evelyn launched in without any greeting. "How do you expect the Treasure Chest to make any money if you keep giving everything away?"

"Giving what away?" Laurie looked up at her wide-eyed. She often forgot how tall Evelyn was. And at the moment she was dead serious.

"Well, pants for one thing, those pants you and Virginia gave to that man with all those kids."

"That man needed those pants." Laurie wished Virginia were there to back her up. She looked around and noticed Anne listening from the other side of the kitchen. "He's the kind of customer we *should* be helping. What's the difference whether we give someone who needs them a pair of pants once in a while, or Mother Barbara gives them money for groceries? It's all the same."

"Well, there won't be any money for groceries if you keep giving away all our merchandise."

"What *all?* What else are you talking about?" Laurie stood up straighter and put her hands on her hips.

"All those books you gave to that professor from the college. She could have paid for those books."

Chase had come back into the kitchen to see if Laurie needed help with the coffee, and Laurie glanced his way. He saw the angry expression on the two women's faces and returned to the parish hall.

"Oh, come on Evelyn," Laurie said. "I gave her half a dozen books, to save her students some money.

What's that, three dollars, since we were selling them for half price?"

"I heard it was more like twenty books. And no one authorized you to declare a sale on books anyway."

Laurie rolled her eyes and turned away, reaching for a paper cup. She was sure Carol had agreed to the sale, but didn't want to stand there arguing with Evelyn about it. The kitchen had grown quiet, and Laurie knew a few more people were listening in.

"And those weren't the only books," Evelyn continued. "You gave a lot of books to the Friends of the Library."

"It wasn't a lot." Laurie said through gritted teeth. "Carol agreed they were books we were never going to sell anyway. We don't have room to store things that we're never going to sell."

"Yes, but those books were antiques. They were valuable," Evelyn insisted.

"Did you even bother to find out anything about them? For your information they were *not* valuable."

Mary entered the kitchen and stood beside Laurie. "What's going on?" she asked.

Evelyn looked down her nose at Mary. "You need to tell your friend to quit giving things away over at the Treasure Chest." She turned and walked away, apparently feeling outnumbered.

"Oh, yeah?" Laurie called after her.

Mary put her hand on Laurie's arm. "Come on. Is this your coffee?" She picked up a cup and steered Laurie into the parish hall where they sat beside Pete and Chase.

Laurie was seething. "That cow. She thinks she owns the place. She needs to remember we are all volunteers over there, or she'll end up running the shop by herself. Which is what she wants, I'm sure."

"She's always been bossy," Mary agreed soothingly. Chase raised his eyebrows and watched silently, taking a bite out of a cracker.

Laurie picked up an apple slice and then put it down again, folding her arms. "Just because she was born with a silver spoon in her mouth, she thinks no one else needs any help. I should just quit working there. There are better ways I can use my time. I'm tired of getting yelled at." She furrowed her brow, feeling the tears filling her eyes.

"You just gotta learn to ignore her. We all agreed to call the Friends of the Library and offer them those books. They were probably never going to sell, like you said. They weren't anything special. Don't worry about what Evelyn says. She's an idiot."

Laurie looked gratefully at Mary. She picked at her snacks, and tried to listen to the conversation around her, but her mind kept going back to the argument with Evelyn – and the argument she'd had the night before with Chase.

As the parish hall started to empty Mary asked, "What do you guys have going this afternoon? Want to go to a movie or something? I can probably get Melissa to babysit." She looked from Laurie to Chase and back again.

Laurie looked at Chase, who shrugged, tossing the question back to her.

"I don't know. We've both been pretty busy, and I've got some work to do. I think we'll just chill and hang around the apartment today." She wasn't sure if she meant herself and Chase in the same apartment or not.

Chapter 27.

Back at their apartment building the two went their separate ways. "I'm not feeling very well," Laurie said. "I think I'll go upstairs and lie down for a while, and then try to get some work done this afternoon."

"Okay," Chase said. "Maybe we'll get together later."

"Maybe," she said. She looked at him, standing there with his hands on his hips, and thought how strong his shoulders looked. She wanted to grab him and hold on for dear life. Instead she turned toward the stairs.

That afternoon Mary called her on the phone. "Hi. How's it going?"

"All right, I guess. Just trying to get a little work done." Laurie had been sitting at her laptop for a couple of hours, but had deleted more than she had added to her latest story.

"Boy, Evelyn sure had a bee in her bonnet this morning, didn't she?" Mary asked. "If she doesn't tone it down she's going to scare everyone away. Like you said, she'll end up running the thrift shop by herself."

"You have no idea how much she irritates me."

"I know. She rubs me the wrong way too sometimes. Just stay away from her."

"How?" Laurie asked, exasperated. "I try to go in to the shop on days she's not scheduled to work, but then she appears anyway! I mean, she's there all the time. It's like she has to supervise us, or spy on us, or something. I do *not* need someone telling me what to do every minute of the day. She just needs to stay away!"

Laurie clearly needed to vent, and it was all Mary could do to slip in an "uh-huh" from time to time. "She is ruining that place for me," Laurie went on. "I mean, I have been working at the Treasure Chest since I got to Chinkapin, just about. I really like most of the other volunteers, and I've got to know some of the customers, and I know we do a lot of good in the community. But Evelyn.... That woman gives me indigestion. I swear, I might have to quit working there."

"Don't say that. We need you. You know we don't really have enough volunteers as it is. Whenever anyone gets sick or goes out of town, we're scrambling."

Laurie let out an exasperated breath, and the women were silent for a moment.

"Did you guys stay in town late last night?" Mary asked.

Laurie snorted. "That's the other thing."

"What happened?"

"Chase and I had kind of a blow-up. Not really, but...an argument, I guess."

"I thought he was kind of quiet this morning. What did you guys fight about?" Mary asked.

"Oh I don't know. He's acting all strange, like he's got a secret. I feel like maybe he's still hung up on Jenny, you know, his late wife."

"Jenny is dead!" Mary pointed out with a laugh. "Jenny is the least of your worries."

"Well, there's this other person I've seen him with. He's been working on some secret music project with her."

"Secret project?"

"Yeah, some music composition thing. Whenever I ask about it Chase gives me some half-baked answer that's not really an answer. And then, he's caught me with Luke a couple of times."

"Wait a minute. Back up. Caught you with Luke? Who the heck is Luke? How did I not know about this?"

"There's nothing to know. I met him in the bookstore in Chinkapin, and I've run into him in the Coffee Pot a few times. Then he showed up at one of my writers meetings in Redding, and from there we went to another bookstore in Redding. Well, Chase saw us leave the meeting together."

"That doesn't sound good."

"Yeah, I get it, but it was nothing! And then I interviewed Luke for that newspaper article, and we had lunch together in Peach Valley, which I let slip to Chase about."

"'Let slip.' Laurie are you hearing yourself? No wonder you're having arguments. I mean, even I think you're two-timing now. What is really going on with you?"

"There is nothing going on! That's what I told Chase Saturday, when we started arguing and he dragged it all up."

"Hmmm," Mary said.

"Everybody's ruining this place for me. Just when I was feeling really at home in Georgia, and Chinkapin, and St. Mark's."

"My father-in-law had another crazy expression that might be appropriate here. 'You shouldn't crap where you eat.'"

"Ew," Laurie said. "I don't even know what that means."

"His original version is a little more colorful. But basically it means you should have thought of this when you got involved with Chase – that if you break up with him now, it could get a little uncomfortable up in the choir loft."

"I don't want to break up with him!" Laurie whined. "I'm just afraid he'll move to Nashville or something."

"Have you ever been to Nashville? It's kind-of a cool place. You could do worse. And you don't really have anything tying you to Chinkapin."

"Oh, now you're trying to get rid of me," Laurie sulked.

"I'm not trying to get rid of you. I'm just showing you that you have options. Listen. You just told me that Chase misconstrued something that *you* did that was perfectly innocent, even though you *have* been all over three counties with this guy named Luke. So maybe, *just maybe*, you're misconstruing something *Chase* is doing that's perfectly innocent. Have you ever thought of that? Good grief, you guys are both so suspicious! I don't know how you could ever stay married to anyone if you're not any more trusting than that. Recognizing, of course, that DB actually *couldn't* be trusted."

"Thanks for that cheering reminder." The two laughed.

"Not everyone is the schmuck DB is, okay? You've been hurt. Chase has been hurt. Time to hit the reset button."

Laurie sighed over the phone. "You make it sound so easy."

"Nobody said love was easy. But the two of you better start talking to each other and straighten things out, or you're never going to get anywhere as a couple. Now put your big-girl pants on. You want to stay in Chinkapin? You want to stay with Chase, and be engaged and whatever else? Well...."

"Well, what?" Laurie was starting to get weary of her friend's unsolicited advice, even if she was right most of the time.

"Well ask, seek, knock, and all that. Maybe you should just...ask."

"I've asked the universe. I'm on hold, waiting for an answer."

Chapter 28.

Laurie didn't even speak to Chase that evening. She spent Sunday afternoon and evening alone in her apartment, which meant she just snacked on cheese and crackers for supper.

The next day she was determined to put her big-girl pants on and at least get some writing work done. She finished her tasks at the *Journal* and then called Professor Abrams and explained her idea for a feature article about collecting old books. Cory was excited to be able to share her passion, and luckily she had some free time, so Laurie arranged to meet her in Peach Valley that afternoon.

Laurie hopped in her car, her stomach growling. The interview was not for a couple of hours, so she planned to stop somewhere for a bite to eat and to write down the questions she intended to ask.

However, her gas gauge told her she wasn't going to make it anywhere if she didn't stop at a filling station. She pulled over at the first one she saw, and started fueling.

Laurie looked around her as the gas trickled into her car's tank, thankful for her jacket. Ordinarily she whizzed past this section of town, but today her eyes lighted on a small sign she had never noticed before: "Evergreen Cemetery .5 miles." An arrow pointed up a road that angled back toward the south side of town.

So that's where it is, she thought. The nozzle in her hand clunked as the pump stopped fueling. She replaced it in its cradle and, on a whim, turned her car onto the side road and drove the half mile to the cemetery.

The first glimpse of the old headstones made Laurie regret she hadn't visited before Halloween. She was sure there was a feature article there somewhere, and was determined to mark her calendar so she didn't miss the opportunity next year.

She drove up the gravel drive under a stone archway and looked quickly around, thankful she didn't see any awnings that would indicate a burial taking place. She parked her car and walked back to read a plaque. The archway dated from the 1920's but she was certain from the style of some of the grave markers that the cemetery was much older.

There was a stateliness and calm about the place. Ancient evergreens and oaks soared over the grounds. Spanish moss fluttered from tall trees. A few old camellia bushes had started to bloom, and others were covered in buds.

Laurie adjusted her scarf, zipped up her jacket a little higher, shoved her hands into her pockets, and wandered among the burial plots. Some were bordered with ornamental iron fences. Others were enclosed by brick or stone. She peered over a low stone fence and read markers dating to the 1830's.

Elegant artwork graced some of the older monuments: large finials, floral wreaths carved in stone, a lamb, an angel. There were relief carvings of doves, oak leaves, and flowers. She walked past headstones, footstones, and slabs over graves; obelisks, arches, and plenty of urns. The elements had taken their toll, but many inscriptions were still legible. Besides the usual "father" or "beloved wife and mother," there were bible verses, tributes, bits of poetry.

The children's graves caught her breath. A few were marked with elaborate headstones listing how many months and days the child had lived. Some stones were inscribed with heart-wrenching sentiments. 'Our darling is gone but not forgotten' and 'Another Lamb has been added to the upper fold of the great shepherd. Another tender flower transported to the garden of God.' Other stones, flush with the ground, were simply inscribed 'Our Baby.'

Laurie snapped a picture of the tombstone of a woman named Mary to send to her friend. The inscription read "As a wife and mother she performed her full duty. As a Christian she hath done what she could." Laurie couldn't help noticing that they had spelled the word "p-r-e-formed" instead of "performed," and she was not sure how to take the inscription. Had this Mary performed her 'full duty' willingly, or begrudgingly? And as for 'she hath done what she could,' did that actually mean she did everything humanly possible, or something like "oh, well, she hath done what she could. It is what it is."

There was the grave of a wife who died at twenty five, of whom it was written "None knew her but to love her, none named her but to praise." Another young wife had died at aged nineteen years and fifteen days. And a woman named Arabella died in 1857 at the age of sixteen years, three months, and sixteen days. Besides wondering how much it would cost today to carve all that detailed information onto a grave stone, Laurie wondered what the girl's life had been like, since she had died so young, but was married even younger. Did she die in childbirth? The stone listed her husband's name, and said at the bottom "We miss thee at home: yes, we miss thee." How precious had every day of the young woman's life been to those at home!

She glanced at the time, and decided she'd better be about the reason she had wanted to visit the cemetery in the first place.

An obelisk inscribed with the name "Anderson" stood prominently in the center of a large burial plot surrounded by ornamental ironwork. *That would have been her maiden name,* she thought. She scanned the grave stones, concentrating on the newer ones, and finally found what she was searching for: the final resting place of Chase's late wife.

It had to be the one, although the inscription bore her maiden name in place of her middle name, Renee. "Jennifer Anderson Harris" was inscribed on the stone, along with her birth and death dates, and the words "God is our hope and strength."

The birth year was two years prior to her own. "My sister's age," Laurie murmured. And as she had discovered on the website, she had died in the fall, just one year ago. Was that why Chase had seemed withdrawn lately?

Laurie looked at the stone again. She guessed Jenny's parents had purchased it, since Chase had told her he had run out of money by the time Jenny died. The location in the family plot made sense, and the inscription seemed appropriate.

The breeze picked up, tugging at Laurie's scarf. She knotted it tighter, took a photo of the gravestone, and returned to her car to drive to Peach Valley.

* * *

The interview with Cory Abrams went well, and afterwards Laurie took a few photos of the professor in front of the collection of old books in her office at the university.

"Thanks again for the books from the Treasure Chest," Cory said.

"Happy to help. If you can give us a list of books you're using in class, we'll keep an eye out for them. And congratulations on your upcoming wedding. I guess it slipped Luke's mind, with the store opening and everything." She smiled as Cory rolled her eyes.

"I guess men's minds don't work like ours," Cory said, "because the wedding sure has been in the forefront of my mind."

"Little things like weddings don't seem to matter so much to guys. I've been waiting for my boyfriend to propose, but I may end up having to ask *him*."

Laurie couldn't believe she had said that out loud to this woman whom she barely knew. She felt herself starting to blush, but Cory eyed her with sympathy.

"You know what they say, 'The course of true love never did run smooth.' Luke and I have known each other for a long time. Unfortunately I was already married, back when we met! We'll have to get together for coffee some time, and I'll tell you all about it." Cory looked at her watch. "But now I have to run to a faculty meeting. I'll walk you out."

Laurie thanked Cory for the interview. On the drive through Peach Valley she mulled over ideas for an interesting lead paragraph for her article about rare and vintage books, but her mind kept jumping back to Cory and Luke. *Their story must be really interesting*, she thought. Before heading out of town she drove past Franklin's bookstore and parked just down the street.

She cupped her hands around her eyes and looked through the store window. Luke stood at the counter inside. He spotted her and waved her in.

"I just had a nice chat with Cory about rare books for a feature article for the *Register*. That's a fascinating hobby she has." Laurie narrowed her eyes and pointed a finger at Luke. "You somehow failed to mention that the two of you are getting married soon. That's kind of a big deal for most people."

Luke smiled shyly in return. "Yeah, well. It is a big deal. I guess we've both been waiting for this for a long time."

"She mentioned you've known each other for a while." Laurie hoped he would say more. She tried an old interview technique she had learned in school: remain silent, and maybe the interviewee will continue talking to fill the void. This time it worked, and Luke began to speak.

"I think I told you I graduated from a liberal arts college in north Georgia. But between my junior and senior years there, I came back to Peach Valley for a summer job and took an evening class at the college here. I wanted to make sure I had enough credits to graduate the following May. Cory was a grad student, and the teaching assistant for the class. She wouldn't even have been here, but she had married a guy from her high school, a soldier, who was off in the desert. When he deployed, she went back to school to keep busy. Anyway, I already wanted to be a writer, and was looking for someone to help polish my work. We just clicked. She really opened my eyes."

Laurie raised her eyebrows.

"Not what you're thinking." He laughed. "I thought I was hot stuff around my college, a real man of letters, but she showed me a thing or two I never knew about literature, and how to read it like a professor." Then he added, "But you're right, she did open my eyes to more than that. We had a thing going all that summer. Even into the fall, I put a lot of miles on my old car driving back and forth to be with her. But at Christmas time her husband came back from overseas."

Luke broke off for a moment as a couple of customers came into the store. "Let me know if I can help you find anything," he called.

He continued in a lower voice. "I'd never met the guy, but I'd seen his pictures. He was a big dude, a body builder-type, and of course they were married and everything. I felt like a schmuck. Here this guy was off fighting for his country, and back home I was getting it on with his wife. So I broke it off with Cory, concentrated on school, and tried to forget about her. I don't think that's what she wanted me to do, but I wanted to do the right thing.

"So, life went on, and I had other relationships. I actually lived with a woman for about three years. But it was never the same." He shook his head, looking thoughtful. "I was back in Peach Valley occasionally. I still had family here. My grandparents passed away, their house sold, yada-yada. Well, I heard from a friend that the house was back on the market, and I came to look into buying it. I was thinking of just renting it out. There are always people connected with the university looking for places to rent, so I knew it would work. But, I ran into Cory – I didn't realize she was living and working here again – and found out what had happened.

"I kind of knew things were a little rocky for them before he ever shipped out. Well, their marriage had never really gotten off the ground, and things were even worse when he came back. He didn't seem like the same person she had married. I'm sure he probably saw some awful things in the desert, but anyway he'd changed, become angry and violent. She stood by him for a while, and tried to get him into counseling." Luke shook his head. "People in the military, sometimes they can't do what they really need to, in order to take care of themselves. Either they can't get the therapy they need, or they're afraid they might be seen as unfit for duty, or whatever. But the second time he beat her up, she called it quits and left him.

"I was sure she had forgotten about me, but I never really forgot about her. When I came back here to arrange about buying the house, we reconnected. It took a while, but everything finally fell into place." Luke smiled now. "We're getting married in December, and I couldn't be happier! I've got my bookstore, I've got the house I love, and I've got my bride-to-be. Life is sweet." He beamed, his mustache curling and his eyes crinkling.

"What a great story," Laurie said. "Not the beating part, but.... I wish you much happiness, anyway."

"Thanks. I hope you'll come to our wedding! I'm a lucky guy. To think it almost didn't come together. When I came down here, the woman I had been living with for a while, Deb, was still kind-of chasing after me, even though we had broken up. Well, Cory found out, and jumped to all the wrong conclusions, like that I just wanted to see her on the side while I was still going with Deb." He shook his head. "It was a mess until we got it straightened out. We both could have saved ourselves a whole lot of grief if we'd just talked to each other. But I guess once you've been burned, or fallen for the wrong person, your head gets a little crazy."

Laurie listened, thinking about how she and Chase had both been burned. Maybe she was making things harder than they needed to be.

Luke seemed to remember something. "By the way, Cory and I are thinking of starting a writers group in Peach Valley. I've had a few customers come in asking if I knew of a group - enough to think some of them might actually show up for a meeting. And Cory says some of her former students have been looking for a way to stay motivated. Once they graduate they miss engaging with other writers."

"Oh, that's great! Let me know when you get things organized. I can write something up for the newspaper. And it's just as close for me to come to Peach Valley for a writers group as it is to drive up to Redding." She looked at her watch. "Speaking of driving, I need to be heading back to Chinkapin."

He raised his hand in salute. "I'll be looking for your article about Cory in the *Register*."

Laurie drove back to Chinkapin thinking about Luke and Cory. She guessed Cory must be several years older than Luke – which wasn't much, in the grand scheme of things. Didn't women statistically outlive men anyway? She truly did wish them happiness.

Who made the rules about who you should fall in love with anyway? Margaret Mitchell had had two husbands, and some people thought Scarlett O'Hara's tumultuous love life mirrored Margaret's own. Laurie tried to remember how she had felt about her ex. Her friends had told her what a great catch he was, but now she wondered if she was ever really in love with him.

People get married for all kinds of reasons, good and bad. The next time, if there was a next time, Laurie wanted to marry for the right reasons.

She tried to untangle the roots of her argument with Chase. For one thing, they hadn't been able to spend much time together, let alone talk to each other. He was busy with work. She was busy helping Mary when Roly was sick. Then she was busy with the thrift shop and her writing group. And Chase was busy with some songwriting and performing.

She loved that she and Chase both had creative pursuits. She was proud of what Chase did, musically speaking. And they needed their jobs if they were going to keep a roof over their heads and food on the table. But they could try harder to make spending time together a priority.

Chase had worried that she and Luke were seeing each other. Well, he was dead-wrong about Laurie and Luke, so probably she had nothing to worry about where that blonde – Charlotte or whoever she was – was concerned.

None of any of it would have been a problem, except that they had both been burned before. They were afraid to trust anyone again.

How long would the crap Laurie had been through with her ex – the running around, the emotional abuse, all of it – cast a shadow over her life and keep her from being happy?

"No more," she said aloud.

Chase's late wife had been up to some bad stuff, so it was no wonder he might have trouble trusting someone. If he was worried about whether Laurie really cared, well she would set his mind at ease about that.

Chapter 29.

Laurie went through the motions at work the next day, but she still had her mind on Margaret Mitchell, and Luke and Cory, and herself and Chase.

If Chase hadn't mentioned meeting with Charlotte it was because it wasn't worth mentioning. Sometimes he just forgot things, like when he forgot to tell her he'd agreed to play at the Coffee Pot on Halloween. How did he say it? He was living too much inside his head. Laurie sure wished DB had lived in his head, instead of constantly nitpicking, criticizing her housekeeping, and belittling her writing ambitions. How he had beat her down! Thank God Chase was not like that.

Laurie put it all out of her mind. She finished her work at the newspaper, stopped in the grocery store for a ready-made salad, and drove to the Treasure Chest, hoping Evelyn wouldn't be there. She found Alice working at the counter. "Hi," Laurie said. "I'm surprised to see you here."

"I've always worked on Tuesday," Alice said cheerfully.

Back in the office Joan rolled her eyes. Alice was right. She had always worked on Tuesdays. But she had failed to come on Tuesday so many times in the last couple of months, that the other volunteers never knew when to expect her.

"Well, good," Laurie said. She stashed her purse in the office, and sat for a few minutes to eat her salad and catch up. "Has it been busy today?"

"Oh, you know. People coming and going, as usual," Alice said.

"Is your daughter still visiting, Alice?" Joan asked.

"Yes, she's staying until the weekend, and then she has to go back. Her husband...well, I forget his name. But he called and said to come on home, so she'll be going...wherever. You know, on home!" Judging by Alice's smile, she wasn't upset about her daughter's pending departure. She greeted some customers who came in, and pointed out the day's sales listed on the marker board.

"What is that you're working on, Joan?" Laurie asked.

"Besides making sure Alice doesn't mess with the cash register, you mean?" she asked under her breath. Then in a normal tone she said, "I found this box of shoes and socks that was shoved up under the coats in the back room. I'm going through them, and pricing a few of the nicer ones to put out. When you're done eating you can carry these to the men's room." She pointed to a neat pile of men's socks stacked together. "These others are the ones I haven't found the mates for."

Laurie rummaged in the box between bites, and helped match up socks. Joan talked while Laurie chewed.

"I think all of these belonged to Benson. His son brought in a lot of his things: pants, neckties, shirts, even a couple pair of shoes."

"He was such a nice guy," Laurie said. "He always had something kind to say when the choir came down after the service." She remembered with regret that she hadn't been able to go to Benson's funeral. "And wasn't it shocking almost, how quickly he died once they figured out it was lung cancer?"

"I think they should have been monitoring him better. You know, he had pneumonia last winter, so one would think his doctors would have been watching."

"You know what they say: Life is uncertain, so you better eat dessert first." Laurie finished her lunch and disposed of her trash. She carried the socks to the men's clothing room and dumped them in a large basket. As she tidied up the basket she thought about the average age of the congregation, and who might be next. Mother Barbara had said once that the winter always took its toll on an older parish, and winter was just a couple of months away. Laurie ran her hands over the rack of men's shirts, pulling out a few stray hangers. Then she returned to the office and helped Joan price shoes.

It was a relaxing afternoon. Just enough work to keep them occupied without being harried. A regular customer had brought in a couple of boxes of knick-knacks and kitchen items, and Laurie and Alice sorted and priced them while Joan worked the counter. Then they worked together tagging some blouses.

"What do you think we should charge for this?" Alice asked holding up a cotton sweater.

Laurie suggested a price and handed Alice a blank tag to write on. It was strange. When Laurie first began working at the Treasure Chest, Alice had been the one to tell her what prices to assign things.

Finally it was closing time, and Laurie and Alice walked through the shop shutting off lights. "I know you don't need me to help with the money, so I'll just go on home, see what Don is fixing for supper," Alice said.

"Home safe, Alice." Joan waved absently, and started counting money in the cash drawer. "Can you flip the sign, Laurie?" she asked.

Laurie slid the sign on the door from 'open' to 'closed,' and stood looking out into the parking lot. "It's nice that Don has taken over a lot of chores at home; you know, cooking and things," she said.

"Survival instinct, I think," Joan said, and continued counting under her breath. She punched a number into the calculator. "It's best to keep Alice away from the stove so she doesn't burn the house down. One of these days he'll have to get the car keys away from her."

"I wonder what she's doing out there. It looks like she's having trouble getting her car in gear." Laurie watched through the closed door.

There was a loud revving sound. Joan paused and lifted her head, looking at Laurie. They heard a clunk as the engine engaged, and then a squeal of tires. A second later they heard a loud bang and a grinding of metal.

Laurie bolted out the door, with Joan a few seconds behind her. Alice's car had come to a stop at the back of the lot, the front end smashed against the metal dumpster. The engine was still running.

Laurie looked through the passenger's-side window and called to Joan, "Call 9-1-1. Get an ambulance. She's hurt." Joan ran back inside.

Laurie pulled on the handle, but the door wouldn't budge. "Alice! Alice, can you hear me?" she pounded on the window with her fist, then ran around to the driver's side. She grabbed the car door handle and wrenched hard. It opened with a creaking groan.

Laurie could see Alice didn't have a seatbelt on. The windshield was cracked and the woman sat crookedly in the seat, her head at an angle, eyes closed. There was a gash in the middle of Alice's forehead, and blood streamed down her face. Laurie guessed there would be bruises, or worse, on her chest where she had slammed into the steering wheel. Her purse had been tossed onto the floor, its contents strewn around it. Alice groaned and stirred, but didn't open her eyes.

"Don't move. We're calling for help." Laurie felt stupid, unsure what to do or say. She reached carefully around Alice and switched the car off.

Joan returned, and stood beside Laurie. "It was all so fast," Laurie said. "I'm not sure what happened. I don't know if there was something wrong with her car, or what."

"Maybe she had her foot on the gas pedal, and thought it was on the brakes," Joan guessed. "I've called for an ambulance. They'll be here in a minute. Maybe we should call for a wrecker? Or call Alice's husband!"

"Oh, Jesus, yes," Laurie said. "Did you bring your phone with you? Poor Don." Joan placed the call as Laurie paced back and forth, alternately watching Alice and looking up and down the street. At last she heard a siren, and trotted to the end of the driveway. She waved at the ambulance driver, and then returned to where the car rested against the dumpster.

Arms hugged tight to her chest, Laurie watched while the EMTs checked Alice's vital signs. They levered her gently out of the car and placed her on a stretcher. Joan stood close by, answering their questions.

Don pulled into the lot. He moved more quickly than Laurie thought possible, and stood beside the stretcher. "Is she all right? Where are you taking her?"

Joan placed a hand on his shoulder. "This is her husband Don," she told the EMTs.

A blonde woman walked up beside them. "I'm her daughter," she said simply.

It was decided that Don would ride along to the county hospital in the ambulance, while Alice's daughter followed in his car.

"I was going to call a wrecker," Joan said to the woman. The two briefly discussed where to have the car towed, and the woman left following the ambulance, leaving Joan and Laurie standing in the parking lot looking after them.

They returned to the shop together. Laurie and Joan sat in the office while Joan looked for a phone number for a wrecker and placed the call. "Poor Alice," Joan said. "Like I said, I think she must have had her foot on the accelerator, and didn't realize it."

"Plus she didn't have her seat belt on," Laurie added.

"She has not been acting right at all. I wonder if there's something else going on with her. Has Don said anything to you?"

"No," Laurie said shaking her head. "But he and Alice have been having serious-looking conversations with Mother Barbara. Which reminds me, I'm going to call Mother Barbara and let her know what happened. She'll want to hear about it if one of her parishioners is in the hospital. We don't know how

seriously hurt Alice is, or if she'll be admitted, but...."
As she spoke Laurie dug her cell phone out of her
purse.

Chapter 30.

Alice's accident was thoroughly discussed at the Treasure Chest for the next couple of days. Several of the volunteers went together to the hospital before Don put a stop to any more visits.

For one thing, although Alice had regained consciousness, she was suffering terrible headaches. For another thing, Alice would not have wanted everyone to see her. The blow to her forehead had bruised her face in a rather ghastly, if non-life-threatening way. And the bruising was not confined to her face. Don told everyone she was not badly hurt, but they were keeping her in the hospital "for observation."

"It's a wonder she didn't break her sternum or a couple of ribs," Laurie told Mary as they discussed the accident before choir practice on Sunday. She sat sideways in her chair and noticed Chase looking at her from the next row in the choir loft. "What?" she said.

"That's probably the least of her worries."

"What's that supposed to mean?"

"Nothing," he said, shaking his head. But he continued to look at her somberly.

Laurie faced forward in her seat and was silent. Chase sure didn't seem to be as chipper as he should, considering how well everything was going at work. And things were still somewhat tense between them. Maybe the job had become too stressful? Even at Friday's "thanksgiving" feast celebrating his ownership of the HVAC company with his employees, he had not been quite as bubbly as Laurie would have expected. All the employees had had a great time, though.

The choir finished their warm-ups, and gathered in the narthex behind the crucifer. The verger rang the bell calling the faithful to worship, and Steve started playing the opening hymn on the organ. From below in the narthex Laurie could hear his feet thumping on the organ pedals in the loft above them.

The choir processed up the aisle, around the sides of the church, and up into the loft. They were several minutes into the service before everyone could sit down. Laurie took a moment to scan the congregation below, but as she suspected, Don was not there this Sunday.

After the service, as everyone headed back to the parish hall for coffee hour, Laurie stopped in Mother

Barbara's office. She found the priest picking up her stole from the floor where it had fallen off its hanger.

"Have you been to see Alice in the hospital?" Laurie asked. "How's she doing?"

"Not good." The priest shook her head and repeated, "Not good."

"I saw her in her car right after the accident. It was hard to tell how badly hurt she was. I guess maybe she got banged up worse than we thought."

"Oh. Well...I don't know about that."

Laurie wrinkled her brow, confused. "The accident is what put her in the hospital! Unless.... Unless there's something else I don't know about."

Mother Barbara paused and looked at her for a moment. "She's of a certain age. The body doesn't always cooperate as we get older. I may visit the hospital again today, or just call and talk to Don or to Charlotte."

"Charlotte," Laurie repeated.

"Alice's daughter."

Suddenly a lightbulb went off. "There was a woman with Don when he came to the Treasure Chest, just after the accident," Laurie said.

"That's right."

They were interrupted by another parishioner who needed to talk to Mother Barbara. Laurie made her way back toward the parish hall, deep in thought. *Could Alice's daughter be the Charlotte who called Chase the other day?* she wondered.

She walked slowly down the hall and saw Mary in the nursery, leaning over Ricky who was on the changing table. Laurie stepped through the door. "I noticed Don wasn't in church today," she said.

Mary looked up. "He's probably at the hospital. Hey, some of the women took food to their house last week. I wonder why they didn't call me."

"Isn't there a list or something? Maybe it's just not your turn to bring food? Come to think of it, I doubt my name is even on the list."

"Maybe I'll make a casserole, or lasagna or something, to take over," Mary said. "Or maybe a restaurant gift card would be better."

"Mother Barbara just said Alice's daughter from Alabama is still here. Her name is Charlotte, she said." Laurie still looked puzzled.

"Yeah, that's what Tracy said her name was. I'm not sure I've ever talked to her, but I guess I've seen her a few times."

"I'm heading to the parish hall. Are you and Pete staying for a while?"

"No," Mary said, stuffing items into the diaper bag. "We need to get this little man home for lunch.

Then hopefully he'll take a nap, and then maybe Pete and I can take a nap." Mary grinned.

"Enjoy your nap." Laurie made air quotes, and smiled. She stopped in the kitchen, glancing around to make sure Evelyn wasn't there, and then emptied the last of the coffee into a paper cup. She found Chase in the parish hall engaged in a lively discussion about some band or other with a few of the choir members. She listened as the talk went back and forth. Finally people started to disperse and she and Chase were left alone at the table.

"What say you? Shall we head home and fix some lunch?" Chase asked. "Or maybe we'll go out for a pecan waffle." He reached over and twirled a lock of her brown hair around his finger.

"I don't know. I wonder how crowded the restaurants will be." She took his hand and held it. Then she blurted out the question that was on her mind. "I stopped to ask Mother Barbara about Alice, and she said something about Alice's daughter Charlotte. That wasn't the Charlotte you were talking to the other day, was it?"

Chase raised his eyebrows. "I've talked to her a couple of times, yeah." He sat back in his chair.

"What about?" Laurie asked. She looked him directly in the eyes.

"I told you, it was about some music for a special church service."

Laurie waited, hoping he would say more.

Chase let out a sigh, leaned his arms on the table, and looked at Laurie. "She commissioned me to compose something. That's the song I've been working on. I haven't worked out the details yet. I guess I'd better spend some time on it today though. And now, you have to answer my question: home, or pecan waffle?"

"I vote for the waffle," Laurie said.

Chapter 31.

After working at the *Journal* Monday morning, Laurie spent the afternoon polishing a short story. She had read about a fiction contest, and had something which pretty much met the criteria for submission, so she wanted to fix it up and send it off.

A few hours later she scampered down to Chase's apartment to help with supper. They worked together and made small talk, chatting about random, unimportant topics. Each had been walking on eggshells around the other, not wanting to argue anymore.

While they ate Laurie finally got up the nerve to ask, "Chase, do you like it here in Chinkapin?"

"Yes. I like it here a lot." He had a puzzled look on his face. "If I didn't, I wouldn't have worked so hard to buy out the HVAC business. Why?"

"No reason."

"Do *you* like it in Chinkapin?" he asked.

"I love it here. I've made a lot of friends, not counting Evelyn, who I wish would drop in a hole and disappear. And I like my job, and all the free-lancing I'm doing. I like the writers group in Redding, and I like St. Mark's. I'm not planning to go anywhere. It would sure tick off my brother, after he dragged all my stuff six hundred miles down the freeway."

"Look, Laurie. I'm sorry we had that argument the other day," Chase said. "I've been wanting to apologize. I know there's nothing going on between you and the guy with the funky mustache."

"Luke. His name's Luke Morgan. I better not let you address the card. 'Best wishes to Cory and the guy with the funky mustache.'"

"Why are we getting him a card?" Chase asked blankly.

"For their wedding." Chase still looked blank. "Luke and Cory. They're getting married in December, and we're invited."

"Oh!" Chase seemed surprised and relieved. And then puzzled. "Do I know Cory?"

"Cory! The professor who told us about our *Gone With the Wind* book. I mean us at the Treasure Chest. Come to think of it, I guess you haven't met her, but she's the one I wrote the article about, the one about old books. You read my article, didn't you?"

"Uh...." Chase looked down at his food, up at Laurie, and back at his food again.

"I guess not," she said, amused. "And I had a lot of compliments on that article."

"Well, we've both been pretty busy lately."

"I'll agree with you there." She smiled ruefully at him. "Cory was with Luke the day I went to interview him in Peach Valley. He told me that she could evaluate the copy of *Gone With the Wind* we had, since she's an expert on old books, and she came to the Treasure Chest to check it out. That's actually when I found out they were engaged. Later I interviewed her for the article, and was invited to the wedding."

"Ah. Makes sense, I guess."

"We really do need to talk to each other more! But tonight I need to finish my story so I can send it off. Maybe you can bring your guitar upstairs for a change."

* * *

By Tuesday when she hadn't heard any news about Alice, Laurie called her friend Mary at the Treasure Chest. "Who's working with you today?"

"Just Joan. We've been sorting through bags of clothes looking for more winter clothes for kids."

"Well, if Evelyn's not there, maybe I'll come over for a couple of hours this afternoon." Laurie drove to the thrift shop after lunch, and found Joan and Mary idling at the counter.

"So where's Evelyn been lately?" Laurie asked. "Usually she's in here every time I turn around."

"You haven't heard?" Joan said, her eyes looking especially large behind her glasses. "That little Maltese rat of hers, Duchess, was attacked by a hawk."

Laurie's jaw dropped. "Oh my God. You're kidding."

"Not kidding. Anne told me all about it. Evelyn and Duchess were out in their driveway when a hawk appeared out of nowhere and tried to carry the dog off. It ripped a gob of fur out of the dog's back, and clawed one of its hind legs pretty badly. Evelyn screamed and grabbed for the dog, and the hawk dropped it. Anne showed us pictures. It did look a little worse for wear."

"So what happened to the dog?"

"Oh, it got a few stitches in its leg, and it'll wear a 'cone of shame' for a while. But of course Evelyn treats that dog better than she treats her offspring. She's nursing it and keeping it indoors as much as possible. Poor little mutt. I've heard of that sort of thing happening before, but never around here."

"She doesn't live out in the country or anything, does she?" Mary asked.

"No, but she's in a newer subdivision where all the lots are really big. I think the whole place was a peach orchard about ten years ago."

"I'll have to tell Chase about this," Laurie said. "He wants to get a chiweenie, after seeing that one at the pet blessing."

"Maybe he should wait until he has a yard," Mary said.

"I kind of think so too." Laurie changed the subject. "Hey, has anyone heard anything about Alice?"

"We still don't know whether she's out of the hospital," Joan said. "They sure are keeping her a long time, considering Don said the accident wasn't that serious." She pushed her glasses up her nose and pointed out the window. "That's Mother Barbara's car across the way, and I believe the other one is Don's. We've been waiting to see if anyone comes out of the church office. If I didn't think I would interrupt something, I'd be real nosy and run next door and see what's going on."

"You might as well. You won't miss anything over here. It's been a slow afternoon," Mary said. "We did have someone drop off a box full of Christmas stuff. We already priced everything and put it out in the Christmas room. And we've been going through some bags of clothes. Come look at this cute navy-and-white dress I found. It's snug around my waist, but it might be perfect for you."

Joan plugged in the little vacuum and started sweeping while Laurie and Mary went to look at clothes. Laurie tried on the dress, and bought it and a pullover top she found as they sorted through another bag of clothes. Finally they took a break from tagging things and returned to the office to sit and talk to Joan, who was back at the counter.

"They're still at it across the way, huh?" Laurie said, seeing the cars across the parking lot.

"Yep. It's got me worried they're talking so long. Unless that's not Don's car after all," Joan said.

"If you think you two can handle things, I'll go pick up Ricky and get on home to think about supper," Mary said.

"Not a problem, Mary," Joan said. "You just skedaddle."

Laurie walked out to Mary's car with her, and looked across the lot toward the church a moment before returning to the shop. She busied herself tidying up a rack of shirts and blouses, re-hanging items that had slipped off the hangers, and plucking out the empty ones. A moment later the bells on the door jangled.

"Hello, Don," Joan said. "I thought that was your car across the way."

Laurie walked over to join them as Don sank into the chair opposite the counter. He looked "wasted," as she would have said in her college days – washed out and exhausted. "How's it going? You look like you could use a vacation. Is Alice coming home anytime soon?"

Don closed his eyes a moment. Finally he opened them again and said, "Alice is not coming home. Not soon, not ever."

Laurie held her breath. *Not coming home.* Did that mean maybe going to a rehab facility? Or....

"Oh, Don, I'm so sorry," Joan said.

Don shook his head and waved her off so he could continue. "This all started months ago. You remember the robbery here at the Treasure Chest, when Alice got hit on the head. It wasn't long after that she started being forgetful."

Joan nodded, afraid to interrupt again.

"I should say *more* forgetful," he added with a weak smile. "Normally if you have memory problems from a blow to the head, like she did, you recover

over time. But she got worse. I convinced her to ask her doctor, and he finally ran some tests." Don paused. "Well, we were thankful when they decided it wasn't Alzheimer's. They called it a mild cognitive impairment, maybe caused by a mini-stroke. And they gave her some medicine for her blood pressure. She's always lived pretty healthy and stayed active and watched her figure. But high blood pressure or heart trouble can be genetic. If you have it, you have it.

"So, we kept an eye on things, but she wasn't improving like she should have after a mini-stroke. Then her doctors ordered an MRI, and they decided she must have had what they call a silent stroke. Silent strokes don't necessarily affect your speech or mobility, but they do kill off your brain cells. And often when people have had one, they end up having *more* than one." He paused again. "When the effects pile up, they call it vascular dementia. Alice wanted it kept quiet. She just wanted to stay active and do everything as usual for as long as she could. She didn't want people feeling sorry for her. The car accident brought all that to an end."

Laurie swallowed a lump in her throat, remembering the sight of Alice in her car with the blood streaming down her face.

"After the accident of course her head was hurting. I thought that was normal, but the doctors found an aneurysm. Then yesterday Alice started really aching and asking for help, and suddenly it was like a fire was lit under everyone. The aneurysm had ruptured." He paused to pull out a damp-looking handkerchief and blow his nose.

"They went in and tried to fix it, but – it wasn't fixed. There were more ruptures. And Alice had clear instructions on file of what she wanted to do if anything like this ever happened." Tears filled Don's eyes and then streamed down his cheeks. He leaned forward in the chair and rested his elbows on his knees.

"Poor Alice," Joan said, and put her arm around Don. She patted his shoulder, and then rubbed his back in small circles, trying to comfort him.

Laurie found it shocking to see the man cry. He had always been so strong and in control. She swallowed again, trying to hold back her own tears.

"I was just talking to Mother Barbara about the funeral. We'll be having it real soon. Of course Alice knew just how she wanted everything. She already had her plans in place, because of the strokes and her prognosis." His voice sounded thick. He sat back again and took a deep breath.

"I hate this for you, Don. I just hate it. I wish I could do something." Joan looked over at Laurie and shook her head. Laurie stood twisting a plastic hanger, blinking and swallowing hard.

"Barbara said we can count on the church women to provide lunch after the service," Don said. "And of course Alice wanted the choir to sing. We hope to have as many of you as can make it." Don looked at Laurie. "Charlotte already asked Chase to come up with something special, because Alice just loved his music, and his voice. Charlotte has handled all the particulars of that."

Laurie nodded slowly, running over everything in her mind. Charlotte had asked Chase to write music for a special service – her mother's funeral. And Alice hadn't wanted anyone to know what was happening to her. Finally Laurie understood the secrecy, the mysterious meetings, and the phone call. She wondered how long Chase had known that Alice was dying and wasn't able to tell anyone about it.

She closed her eyes, and this time could not stop her tears from falling. Chase had never given her a reason to doubt him. It was all self-doubt and leftover anxiety caused by her stupid, hateful ex-husband. She twisted hard on the hanger, and it snapped in her hands.

She had missed the question Joan just asked, and tried to figure out what Don was saying. "Forty years. Actually, it's forty-two years we've been in this church. She's led the altar guild, and the church women's group, worked on Christmas pageants and Easter egg hunts – everything. This church has been such a big part of her life. And mine."

"Are you going to tell everyone, then?" Joan asked.

"Mother Barbara said she'd email something to the parish. But would you please pass along what I've told you to the Treasure Chest volunteers?" Joan nodded. "And Charlotte is getting hold of the other kids and family. She's been a real comfort through all this. I don't know what I would do without her."

With another big sigh Don rose from his seat, straightened, and walked out the door squinting against the afternoon sun. Laurie watched him cross the parking lot and drive away, and then slid the sign down from 'open' to 'closed.'

Chapter 32.

Joan pulled all the bills and coins out of the cash drawer and laid them in piles on the check-out counter. Laurie walked slowly through the shop, turning off lights as she went. When she returned to help Joan count the money she found her cursing under her breath. "Damn. The money will not match up with the receipts!" She slammed her hand down on a pile of one dollar bills. Tears slid down her face.

Laurie placed her hand over Joan's. "It's just awful, isn't it?"

"Yes! It's awful." Joan sniffed. She pulled a tissue out of her pocket, removed her glasses, and smeared the tears from her cheeks, along with a quantity of makeup. "I've known Alice ever since I joined St. Mark's. She was one of the ones who got this thrift shop off the ground." She blew her nose. "And it's not only that. I can't tell you how many people I've known just in this church who are gone now." She started naming names.

Though Laurie was still a relative newcomer to the church, she'd heard many of the names Joan mentioned, had seen their photographs on the parish hall bulletin board. People who had lived, and loved, and served in the church. They had been married at St. Mark's. Their children and grandchildren had been baptized there. They carried the cross in the procession, bore the chalice, sang in the choir. She thought of Benson, whose belongings they had sorted through and put out for sale not long ago, and her throat tightened.

"Well, me standing here bawling is not going to get the deposit figured out." Joan looked hopelessly at the pile of cash, and Laurie helped her start the count over again. They were off less than a dollar this time, and made up the difference with change donated by a customer.

The two left the shop together, and Laurie made the short drive to her apartment on autopilot, thinking about Alice. She had been one of the first Treasure Chest volunteers Laurie had worked with, besides Mary. *And Mary doesn't even know yet*, she thought.

She wheeled into a parking space and let herself into Chase's ground-floor apartment. It was late, and he was already home. She found him in the small living room. His guitar stood propped against the couch, but he was on his feet staring out the window. He turned to face her as she closed the door.

"I saw Don at the Treasure Chest this afternoon," Laurie said.

Chase nodded. "I talked to him too."

"The song you've been working on is for Alice, isn't it." Laurie said. "That's the special music Charlotte talked to you about."

He nodded again, and ran a hand through his hair. Laurie put her arms around him and held him close.

Finally he pulled away. "I really wanted to talk to you about it, but they were so adamant they didn't want people to know about her condition, and that Alice was planning her own funeral. I never dreamed she would need the music this soon. She just wanted to get her wishes down in writing and everything settled before she got any worse."

Laurie took his arm and led him to the couch where they both sat. Chase leaned his head back, squeezing his eyes shut. "This has triggered all the feelings I had last year, when Jenny died and the funeral happened, and everything I went through during that whole time. Our whole marriage was a rollercoaster. Things were great, then things were not great, then Jenny was in rehab, but by that time I was so done. I was so tired of her shenanigans, I actually prayed that she would die. Or disappear. I just wanted her gone from my life." Laurie listened in silence. "Then she came home, and fell in with that crowd again. And then when she actually did die...." He took a deep breath and let it out. "I guess this stuff is never any fun."

He leaned over to pick up his guitar and strummed a few times, tuned one of the strings, and then began playing the melancholy tune she had heard him working on for the past several weeks.

He played it through, looking alternately at the fretboard and gazing into space. "I can't get the words right. Charlotte gave me some words to start with, and told me sort of what she wanted, but I'm not that happy with it."

"Well, let's hear what you've got," Laurie said. "Maybe I could help you."

Chase sang as he played.

Our life is like a leaf upon a stream –
It glides away.
We fade, forgotten, like a dream
That flies with morning's ray
But we are blessed; Oh, we are blessed.
We wither like the flowers and the grass

that burn away.

He strummed and said, "I need another line here.
And then the B section comes in." He continued:

I heard a voice from heaven – "Go in peace;
"And rest from all your labor; go in peace;"
The glory and the tomb,

"The something and the something. And then the
A section comes back."

The sadness, and the pain, all the tears,
will fade away
The restless feet, the weary hands
are stilled at end of day
So go in peace; Oh, go in peace
The memories, the laughter, and the love
Will carry on,
Our lives and hearts enriched by those we knew
But now are gone.
And we are blessed; We all are blessed
So go in peace; go in peace.

He looked at Laurie, and the expression on his
face melted her heart. "You know, it's not just Alice.

And it's not really about Jenny – I was over her a long time ago. Her dying was a relief. But it makes me think. It's like they talk about, the ones we love but no longer see: my grandpa, a friend of mine who died in a motorcycle wreck...."

"I know. Joan and I were talking about that at the Treasure Chest: all the people we knew who are gone."

He sighed heavily. "Anyway, I've got to get this song finished. They're going to need it soon."

"Maybe we can work on it together. I think it's pretty good already, but...is there a way you could make the tune a little less sad? Because the words are actually sort of hopeful. Where's your notebook?" She found Chase's notebook and pen on the table. "Play it again for me."

Chapter 33.

St. Mark's nave was nearly full late in the morning the following Saturday. People rustled leaflets and prayer book pages. They turned to see who was already there, and who was just arriving. Family and friends greeted one another and made room for one or two more in their pew. They admired the flower arrangements placed around the urn holding Alice's cremains, and handed around boxes of tissues.

Laurie and the rest of the choir sat in the loft, clutching prayer books and watching the congregation. Then the verger rang the bell. The candles on the altar flickered as a breeze moved through the lofty sanctuary. Laurie heard a soft tread in the aisle below, and the crucifer came into view carrying the cross, followed by Mother Barbara. With a rushing sound everyone got to their feet, and then the church grew silent again. An old man with a creaky voice said, "I can't see. What's happening?" and was shushed by the woman beside him.

"'I am Resurrection and I am Life, says the Lord.'" Barbara began, speaking the words of the burial service. "'Whoever has faith in me shall have life, even though he die. And everyone who has life, and has committed himself to me in faith, shall not die for ever.'

"'As for me, I know that my Redeemer lives and that at the last he will stand upon the earth. After my awaking, he will raise me up; and in my body I shall see God. I myself shall see, and my eyes behold him who is my friend and not a stranger.'"

Laurie's throat tightened. She looked at her prayer book, reading the words again. *I myself shall see, and my eyes behold him who is my friend and not a stranger.*

"'For none of us has life in himself, and none becomes his own master when he dies,'" Barbara continued. "'For if we have life, we are alive in the Lord, and if we die, we die in the Lord. So, then, whether we live or die, we are the Lord's possession. Happy from now on are those who die in the Lord! So it is, says the Spirit, for they rest from their labors.'"

The procession had reached the front of the nave. Barbara explained a bit about the Episcopal burial service, for those visitors who were unfamiliar with it. Laurie felt like a newcomer too, and kept a finger in her prayer book.

More prayers followed, and then one of Alice's granddaughters read from the Bible in a clear, calm voice. Laurie wondered if she would be able to read as calmly at her own grandmother's funeral.

The choir and congregation sang a setting of the twenty-third psalm, Mother Barbara read from the gospel of John, and there were more prayers. Then Barbara continued: "Father of all, we pray to you for Alice, and for all those whom we love but see no longer. Grant to them eternal rest. Let light perpetual shine upon them. May her soul and the souls of all the departed, through the mercy of God, rest in peace. Amen."

The exchange of the peace was a bit awkward. Parish members greeted each other as usual, but visitors seemed confused as people milled about the nave hugging or shaking hands. Laurie heard a hollow reverberation, and turned to see Chase lift his guitar from its case and carry it to the front of the loft. The sopranos made room for him next to the organ. Chase swung the guitar strap over his head and gently brushed the strings, though he knew the instrument was still in tune. People in the nave finally returned to their seats.

He sang the requiem he had been working on for the past two months, though he had modified it to make it less gloomy, and more hopeful. His voice was clear and warm, smooth as liquid. Laurie closed her eyes and listened. The ministers at the altar quietly moved back and forth, preparing for communion, but the congregation was spell bound. Don and members of Alice's family had turned in their seats and watched Chase in the loft. Laurie wondered if he were truly as calm as he appeared. The final guitar chord hung in the air and slowly faded.

At last the spell was broken by Mother Barbara. "We are mortal, formed of earth, and to earth we shall return. All of us go down to the dust; yet even at the grave we make our song: Alleluia, alleluia, alleluia."

The rest of the service went by in a blur. The choir sang more hymns than usual, due to the large crowd taking communion. Barbara said the concluding prayers, and Laurie re-read them to herself, thinking of Alice. *Receive her into the arms of your mercy, into the blessed rest of everlasting peace, and into the glorious company of the saints in light.*

Everyone was invited to move out into the columbarium courtyard for the brief burial service. The choir remained in the loft, and Steve played a somber prelude on the organ as people filed slowly out through the various doors and took their places.

Laurie couldn't clearly see or hear what was going on. "What's she doing?" she whispered.

"Mother Barbara's placing Alice's ashes in the courtyard garden," Mary whispered back. "Then she'll sprinkle dirt over the ashes, and then the family can strew flowers over the new grave."

After a few moments there was a final "Amen" from the group in the courtyard. Steve played an elaborate recessional on the organ, and the crowd began to disperse. A few headed for their cars in the parking lot, but most wandered back towards the parish hall where the women of the church had prepared a reception.

As members of the choir chatted quietly and shrugged off their robes, Laurie walked over to Chase. He put his guitar in the case and snapped the lid shut. Then he rose, and Laurie softly kissed his cheek. "That was beautiful, Chase."

He wrapped his arms around her and held her close, leaning his head against hers. "I'm just glad it's over." Then he looked into her eyes. "Thanks for your help."

"No problem. We make a good team," she said.

"We do. A very good team." He gave her a lingering kiss.

A few other choir members came to tell Chase how much they liked his song. "Can I commission something for my funeral?" Steve asked. "Not that I plan to go anytime soon, but...." He shrugged. "You never know."

Laurie carried her things down to the robing room where Mary was hanging her surplice. "Poor Alice," Mary said. "And poor Don. It was a beautiful service, though."

"It was nice," Laurie agreed. "That's the first time I've been to a funeral here. And there sure was a crowd, wasn't there?"

"Yes. They have a big family. Of course, they weren't all relatives. Alice never met a stranger, and you saw that nice obituary. Word got around town after she had the accident." Mary sighed. "I just hope we don't have too many more funerals. You know, it's getting to be that time of year."

Mary's husband Pete stopped in the doorway. "You ready to go? We told the babysitter we'd be back soon."

"See you." Mary waved to Laurie and left with Pete.

Laurie hung her surplice and cassock, pondering what Mary had said about the time of year. She had been in Georgia for less than a year, but so much in her life had changed. She had moved here just after her divorce was finalized, feeling that a part of herself had died with her marriage. Now she felt like her whole life was ahead of her. And yet, Alice's mortal remains had just been buried in the courtyard. *In the midst of life we are in death.* She had just read those words in the prayer book, and it was true. A pall seemed to hang over her. Suddenly the small room felt oppressive.

"Are you coming to the parish hall?" Chase said.

"Oh! I didn't hear you come down from the loft. Yes." She took his hand and he led her back through the church and down the hall.

For casual church gatherings, food was always laid out in the kitchen, but today tables covered with white linens were arranged in the center of the parish hall. Church women walked to and fro bearing plates of hors d'oeuvres, finger sandwiches, and extra napkins. Hot coffee and iced tea occupied the end of one table where Carol stood filling plastic cups with ice.

Alice and Don's family and friends gathered at tables around the room's periphery. Some talked quietly about lost loved ones. Others chatted and laughed in that curious mixture of grieving and reunion that always attends a funeral. A few kids ran back and forth playing keep-away with someone's toy.

"I'm dying of thirst. How about you?" Chase asked.

"I could use some iced tea. It was hot in that loft this morning."

Chase grabbed a couple of plastic cups filled with iced tea, and the two went to mingle. Several people shook Chase's hand or hugged him, thanking him for the song. "It sounded great," Don said. "Alice would have loved it."

Laurie walked up to Charlotte and offered her hand. "I'm Laurie Lanton," she said. Charlotte was an attractive older woman, and Laurie cringed inwardly over her former ill feelings toward her.

"Of course," Charlotte smiled warmly, shaking Laurie's hand. "Chase has told me so much about you. We really appreciate him writing that song and singing for Mom. She didn't want people to know about her problems. She didn't want anyone to pity her, when she felt like she'd been so blessed all her life. She just wanted things to stay the way they were for as long as possible. I know everyone in the church loved her. I'm sure she's smiling down from heaven right now."

Laurie could only nod. Her throat felt tight, and she didn't want the tears to start falling.

Again she found Chase suddenly at her elbow. "I'm not really hungry," he murmured. "Do you want to go somewhere? I feel like I've been at church all day."

She nodded, and the two discarded their cups and left the building without being noticed.

Chapter 34.

The afternoon was warm for late fall, and the sky was a dazzling blue. They walked toward town a while in silence. "That was my first funeral in this church," Laurie said. "It's a beautiful, hopeful service, isn't it?"

"Yes, it is. I had forgotten." Chase talked about funerals he had attended in the past. He struggled to remember the details of Jenny's funeral, which had been held in Chinkapin at the Methodist church her parents attended. "It's something of a blur. Everyone was kind, but the atmosphere of the service was different. She died so young, and, you know, most people didn't know exactly how she died. Of course the family knew, and wanted to keep the details of her drug addiction from coming out. It was just...strange. I left town immediately after the funeral. I mean, *immediately* after; I didn't even stay for lunch with the family. I just ran away from everything for a while. It took me some time to figure out how to leave things behind, what parts of my old life I wanted to shrug off, and what I wanted to keep."

They walked past the Coffee Pot and Chase turned the corner. Laurie had been walking straight ahead, but turned and trotted to catch up with him. "I've never been down this way," she said.

"Yeah, you have. We parked back here on Halloween. One of the guys installed a system in this old neighborhood several weeks ago, and I came with him and checked it out."

They crossed a street where a few attractive old homes had been converted into lawyer's offices. "I guess these are convenient to the courthouse," Laurie said. "Some of the coolest old houses get converted into lawyers' offices."

"Or dentists' offices. Or funeral homes." Chase added.

"Right!" Laurie was thoughtful a moment. "This neighborhood is literally right around the corner from the cafe. I can't believe I've never driven through here."

"Look," Chase said. He pointed to a realtor's "open house" sign. "There's a house down there I want you to see."

Laurie looked at him curiously before they continued along the sidewalk. They slowed their pace to admire the homes and yards. Many of the houses appeared to be nearly a hundred years old, and a few even older. Occasionally there was an in-fill house built more recently, but Laurie was glad to see the builders had respected the style of the neighborhood. None of the houses seemed jarring or looked out of place.

"This must be it, here," Laurie said, indicating a sign in the front yard of a wooden-frame two-story cottage. "Wow. How old do you reckon that oak tree is?" She wondered when the word "reckon" had found its way into her vocabulary, rather than "suppose." Unconsciously she was adapting to her new hometown. She drew her arm through Chase's and together they looked at the house with the "for sale" sign.

"That's a dogwood there," Chase said. He pointed to a tree next to the brick walkway leading to the front porch. Ornamental scrollwork decorated the porch between turned posts. A swing hung at one end, with old roses clinging to a trellis behind it. A small table and wicker chairs stood on the opposite side of a double door.

They strolled up the walk, but turned before reaching the porch steps, and followed the walkway around the side of the house where there was a second doorway. Between the doorway and the gravel drive was a flagstone patio and a garden bench. The patio was decorated with clay pots of chrysanthemums and other fall flowers.

The walkway continued into the back yard where a pergola was built onto the side of the old, detached garage. "Kiwis!" Laurie said excitedly. "Look! Just like at the packing shed." Sturdy vines twined up the stout timbers and covered the top of the pergola. Most of the leaves were gone, but the few that remained were unmistakable.

"And guess what that is," Chase pointed further into the yard at a short, gnarly tree.

"A fig, maybe?" Laurie guessed.

"It is." The yard was narrow but deep. They made their way across the old lawn, past a birdbath to a small garden plot with a few dried tomato plants and evidence of other vegetables and herbs.

"What a cool yard this is," Laurie said, turning to take it all in.

"It could be a lot of work," Chase countered.

"Oh, I don't think so. It's all set up; you wouldn't have to add anything. And I like gardening!" Laurie said. Then she added, "Well, as long as it's not *too* much. But working outdoors is good for ruminating over story ideas."

Finders Keepers

"I hear you," Chase said, sounding unconvinced, but smiling at her nevertheless.

Laurie faced the back of the house, and noticed that a small addition with a screened in porch had been tastefully built on one side. Chase looked at the house appraisingly. "It looks good from the outside, doesn't it," he said.

"I want to see the inside." Laurie's heart was beating faster. She really liked everything she'd seen, and was anxious but also a little afraid to see the rest.

They returned to the front porch and Chase knocked on the screen door. Laurie looked up and down the street. "Chase, listen to how quiet this neighborhood is. And we're not that far from Main Street and the courthouse and all."

He turned to face the street. Two kids rode their bikes, and a young couple walked a dog on the sidewalk. They turned at the sound of the door opening behind them. "Welcome. I'm Chad Houser, Chinkapin Realty." Chad held the door for Laurie. "Come right in."

Laurie stepped through the double doors into the bright foyer. Her eyes lit up when she saw the fireplace in the living room.

"I'm glad you're back," he said to Chase. "I thought I would be alone all day."

"You've been here before?" Laurie asked.

"This is the house I was talking about, where our guys installed the new system." Chase explained. "When I saw the 'for sale' sign out front, I figured you might like to see the place, since we've been looking at older homes in Redding and Peach Valley."

"And good timing, too, because the owners have just dropped their price. They sure hated to move before they sold it, but there was a new job involved. Can you picture your furniture in here?" He held out his arms and turned around in the living room.

"Furniture?" Chase murmured, and Laurie rolled her eyes with a smile. Luckily Chad didn't wait for an answer. He led them from room to room, delivering a running monologue about the house, its history, the current owners' renovations and upgrades, including the new heating system, and how much they'd hated to leave. Chase and Laurie followed, opening cupboards, admiring the old bathroom tile, checking the view from the windows. Laurie ran her hands over the bannister, the mantel, and the counters in the kitchen, which was in the new addition to the house.

Finally Laurie and Chase emerged into the yard again, and settled on a garden bench under the pergola. "I loved that new kitchen, and the little keeping room – which I guess was the *old* kitchen," Laurie said. "And I wasn't expecting a second fireplace."

"How about the bonus room upstairs. That would make a terrific music room."

"Music room! Hey, I saw it first! Well, maybe I didn't, but I was thinking that would be an awesome writer's retreat."

Chase chuckled. "I like the fact that it's been updated. Besides the addition and the new HVAC, Chad said the current owners added insulation and upgraded the electrical system. It looks like a solid house to me."

"I love the charm. I like the high ceilings and the tall windows. It feels.... I don't know, it just feels like home. Comfortable and cozy, and light and airy at the same time."

She looked across the yard at the birdbath nestled among the old camellias. A robin dipped and splashed in the basin, oblivious to the people just a few yards away.

Chase unfurled the flyer Chad had handed him, and Laurie tugged it out of his hands. She read the specs, wrinkling her brow and mumbling. "Estimated mortgage payment.... That probably doesn't include taxes and insurance." She looked at Chase, and continued calculating. "Right now we're paying...."

"Right now we're *both* paying rent," Chase reminded her. "Plus, I've finished buying out the business, so I no longer owe those big payments to Mr. Anderson."

Laurie sat back and her shoulders relaxed. She looked up at the vines spreading above her, and then over at Chase.

"It looks like a wonderful house to start married life in," he said.

Laurie's eyes widened. Then she narrowed them again. "Oh?" she said innocently. "Who's getting married?"

"I hope I am," he answered. A curious expression played on his face as he struggled to hide a smile. Laurie was perfectly still, except for her heart which hammered in her chest.

Chase rose from the bench and dropped onto one knee, taking her hand in both of his. "Laura May Lanton, I want you to be my wife."

For a moment she sat frozen, and couldn't speak. Then she bent and wrapped her arms around Chase's neck and pressed her forehead against his shoulder. Her body trembled and tears wet his shirt.

"Hey, don't cry," he said, folding his arms around her and rocking her gently. "I didn't scare you, did I?"

She lifted her head to look worriedly at him. "Oh, Chase, are you sure? You have to be sure!" She looked deep into his eyes.

Solemnly he nodded. "So sure I'll ask you again: Laurie, will you marry me?"

This time she beamed, and her wet eyes sparkled. "Yes! I thought I was going to have to ask you!" She laughed, and wiped the tears from her face. "But I guess I outlasted you."

"Come on. Let's do another walkthrough."

Chapter 35.

Laurie woke early Sunday morning and looked at the outline of Chase's profile in the dim light. She closed her eyes and breathed deeply, detecting the slight scent of his aftershave. He turned on his side toward her, mumbled something, and put his arm around her drawing her close.

Finally he planted a kiss on her hair, stretched, and asked, "So are you showering down here, or going upstairs?"

Laurie ran a finger over the rough stubble on his jaw. "Upstairs, I guess."

"Okay. Text me when you get out of the shower, in case I fall back asleep." He pulled the sheets around himself and rolled over.

Laurie swatted him playfully on the rear. "All right, Mr. 'in case.'"

She threw on yesterday's clothes, let herself out without bothering to lock Chase's door, and climbed the stairs to her own apartment.

Had he actually proposed to her yesterday? Were they really going to make an offer on that house he'd discovered in the charming neighborhood behind the Coffee Pot? It all seemed unreal. She was afraid if she said anything out loud the spell would be broken, and all her pretty dreams would shimmer and dissolve.

She sped through her shower, but took a little longer than usual on her hair and make-up. *Not giving him any reason to change his mind*, Laurie thought, slipping into the navy-and-white dress she'd bought at the Treasure Chest not long ago. The colors were flattering, and the slim waist fit her perfectly.

She went back down to Chase's apartment, glad to see that he had cooked eggs and grits. She was starving. They'd had nothing but ice cream for dinner last night, both too excited to fix anything. Afterwards, their love-making had been more passionate than ever.

Chase set a couple of plates on the table, and looked up. "You look beautiful, as usual," he said. "Coffee?"

"Yes, as usual," she said, smiling. "I wonder if anyone will be at church this morning, considering everyone was there at the funeral yesterday."

"Good question," he agreed. "It might just be the choir and the altar servers."

"We're nothing if not faithful," she said, taking the cup of coffee he offered.

"Faithful," he repeated. Looking into her eyes, he gently caressed her cheek.

"Always," Laurie said, covering his hand with hers.

* * *

They parked in front of the Treasure Chest and walked across the parking lot to the church next door. Laurie paused outside the columbarium court-yard, noting the flowers where Alice's ashes had been placed. "And light perpetual shine upon them," she said.

Steve was warming up on the organ as they went up the steps to the choir loft. Laurie looked through the bulletin, marking her hymnal with ribbons as choir members arrived one by one and took their seats. Mary was slightly out of breath as she slid into her place beside Laurie.

"Everything all right?" Laurie asked.

"Oh, yeah. Ricky wanted to play this morning. Look how cute he is in that little sailor suit I bought him." She held up her phone, and Laurie admired the picture. "And don't you look cute in your new dress that I found for you at the Treasure Chest!"

"Yes. Thank you for not pricing it too high." She laughed, then leaned closer to Mary and said "Chase likes it too." Laurie had the urge to tell Mary about her engagement, and the wonderful house they'd found right there in Chinkapin, but then changed her mind. She wanted to cherish her precious secret just a while longer. She looked over her shoulder and smiled at Chase in the row behind her, and he smiled back.

"All right, choir. Let's start with a few warm-ups," Steve announced. It was always hard to sing early in the morning and the warm-up was welcome, although Laurie felt well-rested for a change.

"That'll be fine," Steve said finally. "Now if you would please turn to hymn 664."

"Oh, I love this one!" Mary said.

"How do you remember them all?" Laurie asked.

"Just listen to the tune. It's beautiful."

Steve played through a verse. The hymn did have a lyrical, flowing melody. The words were a setting of the twenty-third psalm, but a little different.

The choir joined in and Laurie listened to Chase singing behind her, imagining how lovely it was going to be walking beside him through valleys and through green pastures. Her heart swelled with joy as they sang, and she followed the words until tears in her eyes made the letters swim and blur.

There would I find a settled rest, while others go and come;
No more a stranger or a guest, but like a child at home.

THE END

ABOUT THE AUTHOR

Margaret Rodeheaver writes short fiction and novels for children and adults. She enjoys music, travel, and drinking coffee, and lives with her husband near Macon Georgia.

For information about Margaret Rodeheaver's latest books (and the occasional freebie) sign up for email updates at www.MargaretRodeheaver.com

If you enjoyed *Finders Keepers,*
don't miss *Second Home,*
book three in the Chinkapin Series.

Writers Need Readers

Here are some ways you can support your favorite
authors:

- Leave a rating or write a review wherever you
  share information about books.
- Buy their books from your favorite retailer or
  online store.
- Ask your bookstore or library to stock their
  books.
- Share or create a post about your favorite books
  on social media.
- Recommend books you enjoy to your friends or
  your book club. Word of mouth is still the
  number-one way books are purchased.

www.ingramcontent.com/pod-product-compliance
Lightning Source LLC
Chambersburg PA
CBHW071154100726
47908CB00002B/374